# Mordec
# and the
# Hidden Hand

# THE THRILLING ADVENTURES OF MORDEC THE VIKING

THE THRILLING ADVENTURES OF
MORDEC THE VIKING

BOOK 3

# Mordec and the Hidden Hand

JILLIAN BECKER

Typesetting and Cover Design by
FormattingExperts.com

Published by Gothenburg Books
ISBN 978-1-7327275-4-0

# contents

# Mordec
## and the
## Hidden Hand

*To my grandchildren:*

*Matthew & Aaron Slipper*
*Jessica & Elizabeth Dilworth*
*Sam & Charlotte Westrop*

# the house of the silver shield

'You and your two friends will sail for England on The Good Ship Good,' Adam the Lombard said, pushing his chair back from the work-table which stretched almost the whole width of his counting-house, and looking up through brightly polished gold-rimmed glasses at Mordec, his tall young Viking grandson standing beside him.

Mordec too wore glasses, but of a more robust kind. 'When, Grandad? Not too soon!' he said. He liked being here with Adam, in this country, Italy; in this strange town, Brevis; and in this blue-grey hall, where men did their daily work sitting down.

Six men, three young and three old, all of them dressed in blue, sat on stools counting coins and writing figures in big leather-bound books. They were called Computers and could read, write, add, subtract, divide and multiply. From time to time, each of them would visit one or another of the iron-bound chests lined up against the walls with numbers painted on them. He would stand silently waiting for the Keeper of the Keys to come and unlock the lid. As soon as a book or bag had been taken out or put in, the lid was locked again.

The whole business had to do with books and bags, numbers and locks and keys. Its owner and ruler, Adam son of Mordecai, kept watch over it. He paid his workers well and they served him well. They were all comfortably tubby, the Keeper of the Keys tubbiest of them all. He continually roamed the shed, his tray of keys hung on leather straps from his shoulders, pausing at each table to inspect the computing work, and now and then advising a recount of coins.

Clavi was his name.

Clavi had been working for Adam for seven years. Day after day he carried out his duties gravely, but a friendliness came out of him when the stars came out at night. One late evening, strolling with Mordec round the town square, he'd won the boy's friendship by confiding in him how much he admired and appreciated the old man—whom he called 'Signor Scutargento'. He was, he said, 'vigilant as an eagle, strict as a splint, wise and just as King Solomon, and benevolent as summer rain.'

'Signor Scutargento' was Adam's title in the town because his business was known as *La Casa del Scudo d'Argento*—The House of the Silver Shield—for that was the emblem nailed to the street-side of his counting-house door. Mordec more than once overheard townsmen speaking of Signor Scutargento with great respect, as a power among them, and their praise swelled the pride he felt in having such a grandfather. He'd grown very fond of the old man, who, he'd soon found out for himself, was truly kind and clever, laughed long and often, and had a wealth of knowledge of men and their affairs, in market-places, taverns, shipyards, harbors, citadels, palaces, counting-houses, castles, abbeys, churches and cathedrals.

'It's all arranged,' Adam went on. 'Though I'm sorry to part with you, my dear boy, and every day as I sit here I'll be thinking of you and wishing you back again! But you have promises to keep.'

For a moment the old man's smile faded. It was impossible to say how deeply he felt for the boy, and how painful the wrench would be: but part for a time they must. So when he'd rubbed an eye and re-polished his glasses with a piece of white silk which he kept in his sleeve, he smiled again.

'The Good Ship Good. Yes. Bound for southern England. On arrival there you will be supplied with horses and whatever else you'll need for your few days' journey northwards. You will all three be well armed and I won't insult you by suggesting that such seasoned warriors as yourselves take extra guards. However, if there is a trading party traveling the same way at the same time, you might decide to join it. If all goes well you will reach the East Fenreach and rejoin your people in the region well before the day they sail home for the winter.'

'The Good Ship Good,' Mordec repeated. 'Where does it sail from? And when?'

'You will embark at Genova the day after tomorrow. Now tell me, my brave young scholar-warrior, would you find it impossible to believe or just very surprising if I told you that her captain is a woman?'

'Mmm—quite surprising,' Mordec said, tipping his head back for a moment as he thought about the question, then nodding down at the old man as he gave his answer. He resettled his own glasses high on his nose—though being a good Italian pair they hardly slipped at all. 'A *little* surprising.' That was as much as he'd allow. It was a year and a half now since first he'd set sail for foreign lands with his fellow Vikings from their home in the North, and as he'd travelled far and seen much he felt too seasoned and battered by experience to be *very* surprised at anything.

Adam laughed. 'That, however, is the truth. The Good Ship Good is owned and sailed not by a master but a mistress. An Englishwoman. Her name is Anwid Cogg. In all the ports of Italy the merchants will tell you that hers is the safest ship on the seas. I know Mistress Cogg personally, and I respect her. She's not only a born skipper with an arm forged for the rudder and an eye tuned to the clouds, but she's a businesswoman with as mathematical a head for trade as any in our town.'

In short, he went on, this lady captain was *reasonable*. It was a favorite word of the old man's, and he meant it as high praise. Few women he had known were reasonable, he had told Mordec more than once. The only exception he had ever mentioned before today was his daughter, Mordec's mother, wife of Hauk the Viking. Once, over a late glass of wine he had said softly that she had 'almost broken his heart' when she'd left him to go off with Hauk to 'the dark north', but he hadn't tried to stop her. 'Your father is a man of good sense. I didn't make my own feelings an obstacle to their marriage. And now, as a reward for my bearing that separation, here *you* are, Mordec, as fine a grandson as a man could wish for.' And Mordec had basked in his grandfather's approval until the old man had added:

'And now they have given me another grandchild, and he too a fine boy.' Mordec, who was a little jealous of all the attention his baby brother was getting at home, had thought of saying, 'How do you know he's a fine boy?' but stopped himself.

Now he asked, 'How does she keep her ship safe, the woman captain? Are all her sailors fighting men?'

'Men? Well, there's another thing. They're not men at all.'

'All women?'

The old man shook his head and laughed. 'Try again.' His laughter stopped and his face grew stern as he called out, 'Clavi! Why is that ledger lying there when nobody is working on it?'

'Boys?' Mordec said, when the ledger had been put where it belonged.

'No.'

'What then? They're not monkeys are they?'

The old man guffawed, though keeping his eyes on the coins that were being poured out of a bag on to a table.

'But what's left?' Mordec protested, joining in the laughter. 'C'mon, Grandad, tell me!'

'Your friend Lily would have guessed at once.'

'You mean they're *girls*?'

'That's what they are. But that also isn't *very* surprising to you, is it?'

'No. Not really. Not to someone who knows Lily,' Mordec said. 'But—are the girls such deadly fighters that they can protect the ship better than men or boys?'

'They're trained well enough in the art of self-defense,' Adam said, 'but that's not the secret. I'll tell you what it is. Mistress Anwid has a policy. *To run a ship that nobody would shed a drop of blood to plunder.* She makes sure every raider, wrecker and looter in every port on every coast knows that it wouldn't be worth their while. She carries cargoes of little value, and always loads them in broad daylight. It's a plain, dull, disappointing show for greedy spies. And she'll take no traveler who weighs himself down with luggage of gold or treasure.'

'What fare does she charge?'

'Ah, you ask the right questions, clever fellow, I see how your thoughts run. But you aren't there yet. The answer is—a moderate sum.'

'Then does she take an awful lot of passengers? Will we be crowded tight all the way to England?'

The old man shook his head. 'No. She'll take no more than five or six.'

'But then—how does it pay her? I mean, with cargoes of little value, and very few passengers, and no one paying very much—'

'Ah-hah. Now you've arrived. And here's your answer. She works for *us*, and we pay her very well indeed.'

'What's she do for you?' Mordec half-seated himself on the great oak table and folded his arms, settling to listen, sensing that here was something worth hearing.

'A mystery, eh?' the old man said, his eyes full of amusement behind the lights that glinted in his glasses. He was proud to have a grandson who liked to learn difficult things. It was not something he'd let himself hope for since the boy's father was a Viking and battle must be in his blood, and so—though he would have loved the boy anyway—finding so much of himself in the lad had been a pleasant surprise.

'She carries letters for us.'

'Just letters?'

'Just letters. If anyone stole them they'd have nothing in their hands but worthless scrolls full of numbers. But if she herself delivers them safely to certain houses in London, she takes heavy purses away with her.'

'Yes, I see. The letters tell people in London to pay her. But what for?'

'For the passenger fares paid to us here, and for any paltry cargoes she carries for merchants, and most of all for being our messenger to London. She never carries money with her. Yet she gets it safely where she wants it. You may be interested in how it's done. Because it is interesting.'

That was another of the old man's favourite words—*interesting*. 'You see, the passengers and the merchants pay us before she sails, and in London that sum of money is put into her hands. That sum and more, for other business of ours. The letters tell all. And when she comes back to Italy, she brings letters from them to us. Over time what's paid out here equals what's paid out there. The sums balance each other, we say. Everything is recorded, written down in our books.'

'I've heard of a plan like that before. For travelers on land. It was Sam told me about it—the Red Magician, who helped me find my way to you. And he told me it was an idea thought up by Lombards.'

'He was right. We did. We were told that he thought well of us. And we think well of him. We've heard from the captains of trading ships that his knowledge of winds and tides is often helpful to them. Did you like him? Did you feel you could trust him?'

'Yes!' Mordec said without hesitation. 'Sam likes to know the truth about everything. He tells the truth about himself. He told me that he's not a magician. He tells everyone that he's not a magician, but folk go on calling him the Red Magician anyway. I think what he does is—well, it's more—' he paused to think of the right word and it came to him, 'more *interesting* than magic. I want to meet him again one day.'

'This time I believe you've judged rightly. Though you will make many mistakes—all of us do, especially when we are young. Sam Gaudin—or Sam of the West, as he's also called—is by many trustworthy accounts a truthful man, a thinking man, a man of rare abilities and understanding, and there are those,' he added darkly, 'who will not easily forgive him for that. But as you like him you'll be glad to hear that on her homeward voyage, The Good Ship Good puts in at Sam's island. Now off you go and tell the others. Clavi! A lid to be locked—number fifty-three.'

# a foolish prayer

Mordec went walking with two friends in the fields outside the town in the late afternoon. To passing strangers they appeared to be three boys from the North, all tall, all fair, all dressed much alike, though the one in blue wore glasses. And what they seemed to be was almost true. From the North they came, all three, but while two of them were Viking boys, the third was a girl, an English queen.

She was impatient to get back to her small queendom in England, to start the great task she had set herself—to free her country by force of arms from the rule of the Vikings. Mordec and Gus, the boys she was walking with, had come with her to Italy to help her find her mother, yet they were her enemies. They had stood by her, taken risks to defend her. In many a tight comer they had proved themselves honourable enemies, and she too had acted honourably towards them. But she made no bones about it: 'You might've been my best friend all my life, Mordec,' she had said more than once, 'and you, Gus, might one day have become my husband, but you're both my enemies until there is not a Viking left in England.'

Mordec knew exactly what to expect of her: for a little while yet, on the voyage to England, they would talk and laugh together; and then, not long afterwards, Lily on the one side and he and Gus on the other would be doing their best to hurt, maim and even kill each other.

The prospect of the war didn't in itself trouble Mordec. As a Viking he knew that war was a necessary part of life. He wanted to be a good warrior when the time came—whatever else he might be after that. He had ideas of returning one day to Italy, of learning to be a physician, or a lawyer, and living in a town, in a fine house, as his grandfather did. But these were not plans, only daydreams. Lily's war in England was more certain to come about, if anything could be reckoned certain when all depended on the whim of the gods.

Gus's outlook was different. His only aspiration from childhood, strengthening with every passing year, was to be a warrior and leader of warriors. To him war was all-important, and no war could be of greater moment in his own life than the one which Lily swore to lead against him and his fellow-Vikings, the conquerors and subjugators of many of her people. Yet sometimes when he thought of it, and especially when he woke in the night thinking of it, he felt feverish with a kind of dread; not fear of the battle itself, but of what must happen afterwards. For this coming war must bring him one kind of ruin or another, and victory prove as great a disaster as defeat. He knew Lily would die rather than submit again to Viking rule, so to win the war was to lose Lily. But if she won it, he could no more accept defeat at her hands than she could at his, and they would have to part forever.

Listening on this fine afternoon to her and Mordec chatting as they walked side by side close behind him, he thought as he often did in the light of day, 'It might not turn out too badly after all. Things often turn out in ways you don't expect. And anyway, even if a time is coming when Lily and I will part forever, at least she and Mordec will be separated too.'

'I hope we'll get there,' Lily was saying to Mordec, meaning 'get to England'. She knew how hazardous all journeys were. They had reached Italy and found her mother by luck, daring, cunning and force of arms. A simple, peaceful voyage home seemed a dream rather than a likelihood.

'We'll get there,' Mordec reassured her. 'To Sam's island, and to England. The ship we're sailing on is the safest in the world.'

Gus stopped and turned. 'Your grandfather thinks he should send us on the safest ship in the world?' he asked scornfully, feeling that somehow his Viking pride was being slighted. 'Does he think we need to be coddled like infants?'

Mordec said nothing, though he disliked hearing Gus criticize his grandfather; more even than Gus's need to remind everyone—especially Lily—as often as possible that he was a hero in the making.

Lily, who was as brave as the bravest Viking, said, 'It's *good* that the voyage will be safe, Gus. I can't be bothered with unnecessary battles at sea. I need to get home and prepare for the battle that really matters—against you.'

Gus walked faster and started up a hill with an energy and at a pace that the other two had no wish to match.

'What keeps the ship so safe?' Lily asked Mordec.

He told her what his grandfather had told him: that she carried cargoes of little value and no gold or treasure. 'So there's nothing much for pirates to risk their lives for.' Then he added casually, as though it was nothing unusual to him, that the captain was a woman and the crew all girls.

'All girls? Really?'

'Really, truly.'

They walked on and upwards silently. As they neared the top Lily said thoughtfully, 'Pirates might want to carry off the girls themselves.'

Mordec knew she was thinking of her mother, Queen Gloria. For years Lily had believed that her mother had been carried off by Vikings, only to discover, when they'd found her here in Italy, that she'd gone with them willingly, and had even married one of her captors. Since these discoveries had disappointed Lily's hopes and hurt her feelings, Mordec stifled the answer that rose to his lips about girls being captured if they wanted to be. Instead he told her, 'The girls on The Good Ship Good are taught to fight in case they need to.'

'And we'll be there to help protect the ship,' Lily said. 'I'd fight of course, but it would be stupid if

I died in a battle with pirates. That's not my destiny. Without me, my grandmother could never get the other rulers of England to send a huge army into the field against you. No one can do that but me. Even if the kings and earls could get the fighters well-drilled and fully armed, none of them could put fire in their bellies as I could.'

By this time they'd reached the top of the hill where Gus stood waiting for them.

'I wouldn't mind,' Gus said intensely, looking not at them but at the sinking sun. Its light made all their faces glow, and his seemed self-enflamed as well.

'Wouldn't mind what?' Mordec enquired.

'What d'you think?' Gus replied passionately. 'We're talking about a battle at sea, aren't we?' He turned to Lily. 'If you and I—Lily the English Queen and Gus the Viking—could be slain fighting side by side against a common enemy, we'd meet again in Valhalla, and never have to fight each other.' He turned his face again to the fiery west. 'I wish it could happen like that. I've even prayed for it. Here, now, this evening, I asked the gods to give us our marriage feast.' No sooner had he uttered the words aloud than he regretted them. Yet he couldn't have held them back. On this eve of departure, standing on the peak of the hill with the glow on his face, praying to Odin and Thor, he felt more ardent, more reckless than ever before.

Mordec said with mock surprise, 'So the gods hire out their mead hall for weddings, like my father does ours?'

This made Lily laugh, but her laughter and Mordec's words combined to tease and embarrass Gus. His face turned red as the setting sun.

'Oh, you'd never understand!' he said scornfully to Mordec. 'But you do, don't you, Lily?'

Lily answered with a question of her own. 'Did you say you were praying for me to die before I could set my country free?'

'Yes. You and me. Didn't you see me standing here on this peak with my arms raised?'

'Sorry, no,' Mordec said drily. 'We were distracted by a discussion of the voyage home.'

'Lily?' Gus said, ignoring Mordec. He wanted her to understand and share this vivid moment of his emotion.

She looked at him, but with her eyes narrowed, whether in anger or against the pulsing brightness of the sun he could not be sure at first. Then she said, 'Are you afraid to meet me on the battlefield, Gus?'

'Of course not,' Gus gasped. 'Odds-bods! I'm not afraid of the battle *itself,* I'm afraid of what will happen afterwards. If we win you will never forgive me. And if you win—that could only happen if I've been killed. And Mordec too, I suppose. Unless he runs away.'

Saying which, he turned sharply to face Mordec, his hand on the hilt of his dagger, more than half expecting him to be lunging out with fists or weapon. Gus was certain that such a provocation offered to any other of his Viking friends would have brought a swift and fierce response.

But Mordec was not provoked. In this way—and not only this way—Mordec was unlike the others. It was enough for him to *know* that he wouldn't run away. And he didn't believe for a moment that Gus thought he would. Gus, he could see, was working himself up into a fighting mood.

'You take yourself too seriously, Gus,' he said, and pretended to yawn.

'War,' Gus retorted, 'is a serious matter.'

'So's dinner,' Mordec said. 'Let's go.'

'Yes,' Lily said. 'Come on, Gus. What you're saying—it isn't something we can talk about here and now. Perhaps it's not something we can talk about at all.'

She started downhill.

Gus took a step or two, but stopped and watched her until she vanished in the darkening plain below as she neared the town, its shadowed walls a deepening blue, but its gilded towers brilliantly catching the last light of day. Still he remained where he was, brooding on his dark thoughts. Mordec, also staying where he was, said nothing to interrupt them. He lay in the grass, plucked a blade and chewed it. He took off his glasses, closed his eyes, and felt the sun throbbing on his eyelids. A breeze ruffled his hair. Down in the plain an invisible piper blew notes like water-drops.

'Gus doesn't laugh enough,' Mordec thought, not for the first time, 'that's his trouble. He's not good company. I'd rather be with Sam. He laughs often and never makes grand speeches. And I shouldn't

think he ever prays. He tells you things worth knowing. He's *reasonable* and *interesting*.'

The sun set, the shrill sound of insects filled the
air, but Gus went on standing in the twilight 'Still
nagging the gods, perhaps,' Mordec thought. 'Maybe
he should ask Loki the prankster to send him the
gift of laughter. But the gods never listen anyway,
so why bother?'

# a letter to a pirate

That night Adam held a banquet to cover his sorrow at parting from his grandson with the gaiety of feasting and music. Among the guests were Hengist and Horsa, the two other Vikings who'd come to Italy with Mordec and Gus and had chosen to stay awhile and help the Lombards protect their town against violent onslaught by their various enemies. It was a time when battling armies swept the plains of Italy, and there was a need for the services of a young master of weapons—Viking though he be—and a chance for him to win honour, fame, and reward of gold and treasure; and such was Horsa. And Hengist devised and built machines of war, some fire-spitting, all of them deadly. He liked to think that the mere rumour of their frightfulness helped to keep Brevis safe. His fortune too would grow and his fame spread, he hoped, and one day envoys would come from France, Germany and Byzantium to buy his secrets. But for the present both he and Horsa were loyal to the Lombards.

Adam praised them for this at the feast, before all the company. 'And while I cannot have my own grandson with me, I can console myself with your company,' he told them.

'We'll serve you faithfully,' Hengist said loudly for all to hear.

Horsa nodded. 'Provided this town is not invaded by Vikings,' he avowed, 'we'll work and fight only for you.'

When the guests had departed and Lily and everyone else in Adam's household had gone to bed, and Gus lay fast asleep, full of wine, wrapped in a bearskin under a table, Mordec sat up late alone with his grandfather and they talked of Mordec's return one day to Italy, and the life he could shape for himself with his grandfather's help. 'The House of the Silver Shield can be yours, dear boy, if you want it. But you must understand that the business is not safe and sure. Truth to tell, our very lives here are not safe and sure. Wars sweep the land. Foreign armies come in and seize everything they see whether they know its value or not. Within the country, city fights city. Within the cities, and even within the Church, one great man's party fights another's. Rome is nothing better than a restless battlefield. And we in particular are disliked because the great lords of the cities and the Church borrow money from us and hate us for lending it to them. Usually they will not allow their armies to attack us too destructively because they need us. But sometimes they sit back and watch when mobs descend on our houses to search for gold and coins. When they find none, they burn our houses and we flee from them to settle for a while elsewhere. We are used to uncertainty, of course, and ready to move in a moment if we must.

Sometimes we have time to break up our buildings and take everything with us, but at other times we have been forced to abandon our houses and most of our household goods and take only what we can carry—and always, of course, our skills and reputations. Yet for all the hatred and violence against us, I can tell you with certainty that in this age of suspicion and betrayal, in this country where every man keeps his hand on his sword and looks sideways at every man he passes, we alone are trusted, and that trust is the most valuable thing we own. Some are jealous of us because of it. And much as I'd like to hand it on to you, the business and the trust that goes with it, I cannot happily wish such danger on you.'

'But isn't danger everywhere, always?' Mordec asked.

Adam, though a man of peaceful affairs himself, took some pride in his grandson's 'Vikingness', and he responded with a laugh. 'Truly I have a Viking grandson! Well, perhaps your fierceness is just what the House of the Silver Shield needs. Yes, yes. In your hands it will be safer. The whole town's glad to have your friends Hengist and Horsa here. Hengist's helping to build up our arsenal—and he rushes round the countryside spreading news of it. When I told him I'd heard from all sides how he spread word of every new invention and wondered why he didn't keep some things secret, he said, "Boasting is also a weapon". He's clever that lad, though clever in a different way from you. And Horsa too has made sure that every lord and priest, abbot, monk, friar, peasant, townsman, merchant, slave, servant, housewife, child, scholar and soldier knows that he, Horsa the Viking, is the deadliest swordsman who's ever come out of the dark North. And even though he's still only a boy, no one doubts him!'

'But everyone knows that's how Vikings are,' Mordec said. 'We boast that we're the Terror of the World so everyone will be afraid of us.'

'True, dear boy. And it's also true what you say about danger being everywhere. But some lives are less dangerous and more useful than others. When you have had your share of bringing danger to other lands with your sword, come back to me wherever I am, and learn to be a physician, or a lawyer, or a maker of laws. You could still rule other men, not by force alone but by knowing how to rule justly. In our town the law is more powerful than the judges who apply it.'

Mordec liked that. He wasn't only a Viking but also the grandson of Adam the Lombard. He'd listened to his grandfather and already resolved that one day he'd come back and do something to deserve Adam's pride in him. He was sorry he had to leave the old man, sad for his sadness.

'Of course,' Adam said, 'I might not be here when that time comes.'

'Not here? Where then?'

'I mean, I might no longer be alive. Who knows? I'm old. But that must make no difference to you. You'll achieve great things by your own wits and strength. It's only when you stand alone that you find out what sort of stuff you're made of.'

'I stood alone when I was imprisoned and tried and sentenced to be strangled and drowned.'

'You stood bravely. But didn't you tell me that you had many friends helping you? Gus and Lily chief among them?'

'Yes. They did. They saved my life.'

'One day you will find that you are absolutely alone. When you do, don't expect anything to be easy. And always *think*.'

Turning their conversation over in his mind, Mordec went on sitting at the table for some time after Adam had gone to his room. All but one of the wall-torches and a few candles were burnt out. His head was beginning to droop when he heard something which made him sit up and look round. He rose and drew his sword. Two dim figures appeared in the doorway and began to advance towards him.

'Stop!' he commanded, and was about to shout to Gus to wake and come to the defense of the house when he saw who the two intruders were.

'It's only us,' Horsa said, 'Hengist and Horsa.' They had not gone to their lodgings but had waited in the shadows near the outer door until they were sure that Mordec was alone.

'What d'you want?' Mordec asked, laying down his sword. 'It's late. I'm sleepy. Whatever it is can wait for the morning.'

'You're leaving early,' Hengist said. 'There'll be no time for what we want.'

'Which is?'

They advanced into the circle of light.

'Neither of you looks like a Viking any more,' Mordec said, eyeing them up and down critically, taking in their short hair cuts—Horsa even had his pale locks curled on his temples—and their soft Italian clothes, striped hose and pointed shoes.

'Nor do you,' Horsa said.

'At least I don't dress like a Pope's varlet or a wandering player.'

'At least we're still warriors and not doctors or pen-pushers,' Horsa retorted.

'You can write—' Hengist began to say.

'I thought you'd grown out of despising people who can write. I thought you'd even begun to learn to read and write yourself.'

'Yes, I did, but—you don't understand. We want you to write letters for us,' Hengist said. 'To take home to our folks with you,' Horsa said.

'For you to read to them,' Hengist said.

'I see. So you've discovered some use for penpushing?' Mordec laughed.

'Anyway, what's wrong with the way I look?' Horsa asked. 'Men dress like this in Italy. Not servants and players—rich men. I know the Lombards don't, but noble lords do.'

Mordec shrugged. 'I don't care how you look. Let's just get on with these letters. I want to get to bed.'

He fetched feather and ink, and parchments of hares which his grandfather used for jotting notes, settled himself at a table and took down his friends' messages. They gave their explanations of why they were staying on in Brevis—simply enough that here they would become rich; and they added that they would not forget home, mother, father, and would never lose the Viking pride they had in being warriors, seafarers, and conquerors.

'We have fought battles on sea and land since last we saw you, and we won them all,' Horsa dictated.

'Put that in my letter too,' Hengist ordered.

'If I told you about the cities and houses and the ways of folk here in Italy, you would find it hard to believe,' Hengist informed his father, Hengist the Fisherman.

'So you don't want to tell him what the cities and houses are like?' Mordec looked up to ask. 'Or the clothes rich noble lords wear?'

Hengist's face reddened. 'Just write what I tell you,' he said. 'Tell him I'll bring gold home with me.'

'Say that for me too. Say "I'll bring enough gold and treasure to make you a king",' Horsa promised his father, Harvald the Armourer.

When they'd done, Mordec put the pen into Hengist's hand to sign his name, which he could do since he'd had some lessons in reading and writing from Sam's mother on their way to Italy. Hengist found it hard to read the letter, but worked at it until he was sure enough that Mordec had written down what he'd said.

Then Horsa, who couldn't write at all, took the pen and made a drawing of a sword so like a sword that no one who knew Horsa would doubt it was his own and rightful sign. That gave Hengist an idea. When Horsa flung down the feather Hengist took it up and on a fresh strip of hareskin drew a rough picture of himself as he looked this night, and over the figure's head he again wrote 'Hengist'.

'Now you can't give them a false idea of what I look like,' he said to Mordec.

'Right. This will be a warning to them,' Mordec said. 'They'll know exactly what to expect to see when you come home. But—tell me—if you don't trust me, why're you keeping me up half the night writing messages to carry home for you?'

'You don't have to carry them. Just write them. Gus can carry them.'

'So you trust him more than me?'

'I didn't say that I didn't trust you. If Gus doesn't get home and the letters are lost, you can tell them what we want them to know. If you never get home, Gus will have the letters to give them.'

'And who then will read them to your fathers?'

'We thought your mother …'

'Then you expect at least one of us to get lost on the way?'

'Don't forget to—' Horsa began to say.

But Mordec put his hands over his ears and yawned. 'Enough. Bed now. G'night,' he said firmly.

Hengist and Horsa looked at each other. Horsa nodded at Hengist and Hengist spoke.

'Wait, Mordec. One more letter. Please.'

'Why? Who else d'you owe a letter to?'

'No one. I mean it's not a matter of owing. There's something we want to say to someone.'

'Who? C'mon, don't make a mystery of it!' Mordec's sleepiness made him impatient.

'Olaf,' Horsa said.

'Olaf? Olaf son of Olaf the Shipbuilder? Olaf the prentice pirate? Him?' Mordec asked, with a touch of laughter in his tone.

'We know you were angry with him when you left,' Horsa said. 'And it's true he took the small ship which you found.'

'Which really belongs to all of us,' Hengist put in quickly.

'But he *is* our friend,' Horsa said.

'And you *did* sneak off without asking his permission,' Mordec said, and clicked his tongue and shook a teasing finger at him.

'We want him to tell the others about us, about what we're doing,' Horsa said.

'Then write to them all. Why pick out Olaf?'

'He likes to think he's the leader—at least when Gus isn't there,' Hengist said.

'And you want to soothe his feelings. No. No more. I've written down all your messages. I'll read them to your fathers. Your fathers will tell the other fathers. Everyone will hear everything.'

'Yes, but you know how grownups tell things. We want our own words read to Olaf. We don't talk to each other the same way we talk to our fathers.'

'Gus and I will tell. Of course we will. We'll tell them every single thing that's happened to all of us since we left.'

'But—'

Again the two looked at each other, each saying with his look, '*You* explain.'

Mordec waited, his eyebrows raised expectantly. Then he smiled slowly, and finally laughed aloud, a short sharp snort of a laugh.

'Ah-hah! I get it,' he said. 'You want to do some heavy boasting. That's it, isn't it?'

'Well, what's wrong with that?' Horsa said.

'We want our crowd to know what we're doing, how we're honoured here, that we're getting rich,' Hengist said haughtily. 'You got something against that?'

Horsa pointed both his forefingers at Mordec's chest. 'Don't tell *us* that *you* won't make yourself out to be the *grand hero*.' As he said the last two words he prodded Mordec hard. Mordec dashed the fingers away.

Hengist said through his teeth, 'I suppose that if Sigvald the Skald wants to make a saga about you, you'll tell him "Oh no, please don't do that! *I* didn't do anything special"?'

'Sure! That's just what he's gonna say,' Horsa jeered, and shoved a fist into Mordec's shoulder.

Mordec raised a fist to shove him back, but stopped himself. He remembered there'd been a time, not long ago, when he *had* wanted to be sung of as a hero.

But then in England he'd found that he wasn't one. Not yet, anyway.

He conceded, 'You're right. About Olaf, I mean. I *was* angry with him about the ship. Foal of the Foam,' he said, savoring the name that he had chosen for it.

'So you'll write the letter for us?'

Mordec didn't answer. He continued as if he hadn't heard the interruption, 'But I still think it's stupid of him to want to be a pirate when there are much better things to do.'

He could say this now to Hengist and Horsa because they'd seen for themselves that the world was more full of things to do than they'd even have dreamt of in the desolate North; but if he said it at home where pirates were honoured more than kings, he'd be knocked down or shut in a cage as a madman.

Olaf was the one who'd always had the strongest ambition to become a pirate, and the other boys, the whole village, everybody, admired him for it. Even Gus did, the born leader—so much that he hadn't wanted to argue with him over his wish to help Lily find her mother, and had slipped away without telling Olaf or anyone what he meant to do. So had Hengist and Horsa. Olaf would have found them gone when it was too late to stop them. Brave as they were, all three of them—true Vikings who would never shirk a fight with an enemy—had felt a certain shame in choosing to go with Mordec on a mission of honour rather than with Olaf on a voyage of plunder.

A little of this shame lingered with them even now, which was why they wanted to tell Olaf by letter that they were winning fame and gaining riches, not out of some soft occupation that Vikings would think typical of scented Southerners, but as fighting men in a time of war and a place of danger. They *had to* boast to Olaf.

'So you won't write our letter to him—just because you're still cross with him?'

'Cross with Olaf? I haven't even thought of him since I left home. I'll tell you what I'll do. When I get back I'll go to the cave on the seashore where we always meet and I'll tell all of them everything. I'll praise you to the skies, I promise. I'll make sure that Sigvald the Skald hears it all too, so he can compose a saga about you. But I've written enough tonight.'

They could see he meant it and they turned to go.

But Hengist looked back and said menacingly, 'I know you'll keep your word, Mordec. Or let me put it this way—you'd better!'

'I'm well known for breaking my word, am I?' Mordec said, yawning just when he meant to sound offended. To all of them treachery was the worst of crimes.

'No,' Horsa conceded. He hadn't forgotten that last year in England. Mordec had kept a promise to Lily—not to reveal the hiding-place of a hoard of gold—even though keeping it could have cost him his life. 'Not that he'd had any real choice, of course,' Horsa told himself, 'as it was a matter of Viking honour.'

'We only want you to tell the truth about us,' Hengist said.

'Sure. The truth's good enough,' Horsa said.

'And even better if it's spun out a little,' Mordec said.

They knew he was teasing them again, but contented themselves with his promise. They were smiling as they left the house.

Next day, when Mordec and Gus and Lily were setting out for Genova in Adam's roan-drawn wagon, attended by blue-liveried servants, Hengist and Horsa stood one on each side of the old man to say goodbye.

'Did you give the letters to Gus?' Horsa asked Mordec.

'Gus, have you got our letters?' Hengist asked at the same time.

'I've got them,' Gus said.

'And Mordec—don't forget,' they both called as the horses started.

'Forget what?' Gus asked Mordec.

'Them,' Mordec said, turning back from a last wave to his grandfather, and jerking his thumb over his shoulder at Hengist and Horsa.

Only when the wagon had turned a corner and vanished from his sight, did Adam stop smiling cheerily. He took off his glasses, bowed his head, and wiped his eyes with the square of white silk which he'd plucked from his sleeve to wave to Mordec.

The two remaining Viking boys put each a consoling arm about his shoulders.

# the good ship good

Mordec, Gus and Lily waited on the busy quayside at Genova for The Good Ship Good to finish loading her freight. Lily was secretly full of restless impatience. Gus wore a gloomy look. He could think only of how he was about to be borne away from this time of friendship with Lily towards a time and a place, distant but certain, when they must treat each other as the implacable enemies they had to be. They were both uncomfortably aware that the silence between them signified a change already begun.

Mordec sat apart from them on a low wall, giving his attention to the ship. She was a broad tub of a vessel, almost as wide as she was long, with a raised deck fore and aft, on each of which a number of small rowing boats were stacked upside-down. He noticed that the rudder was placed not to one side as on Viking ships and all the ships he'd ever seen, but centre-stern, and seemed to be permanently fixed in place, which was also unusual. He sat staring at it, and observing the Harbour-Master, who was tall, dark-haired, handsome, with a rich, far-carrying voice and a noble, obliging manner; and—as behoved the lord of the centre of the trading world—seemed to know every language of the earth, for whoever addressed him in whatever tongue, he answered in the same. He was dressed in a blue and yellow costume as rich and ornate as a captain's of the Pope's guard, but with even more gold chains across his breast and even longer feathers in his hat, and an ampler cloak swinging behind him, blue as the sky of Italy on a summer evening.

This *magnifico* was visiting the quays turn and turn about, keeping an official eye on the loading and unloading of the half-dozen vessels in port. When he halted before The Good Ship Good for the third time, he turned to Mordec and spoke to him in Italian. 'Good-day, Signore.'

'Good-day,' Mordec said, rising to his feet to answer such a luminary, who now, on hearing the sound of Mordec's reply, switched at once to his native language.

'You are to sail with the English Captain?'

'Yes,' Mordec said, 'on The Good Ship Good.'

'Captain Cogg,' the Harbour-Master said, 'is her name, Captain Anwid Cogg. What do you think of her ship?'

Mordec looked at the ship again and delivered his considered judgment. 'I think she's heavy. I think she must be slow. I don't think she can be easy to turn.'

The Harbour-Master nodded. 'Captain Cogg believes her ship to be very much ahead of the age,' he said. 'She is convinced that in a hundred years or so, all the freighters in the world will be built like hers. Wide and deep, and with rudders astern. She has assured me that a rudder works better astern than anywhere else.'

'And do you think she's right? About the rudder, I mean.'

The grand official raised his eyebrows, shook his head, and shrugged. 'I cannot say. I've never been to sea.'

'You've never sailed?'

'Not out of the harbour, no. But if ever I do, I hope it will be in her,' he said, nodding at The Good Ship Good. 'The safest ship on all the seas.'

'So I've been told,' Mordec said. 'What's the cargo?'

'Rough stuff. Nothing precious. Garlic, samphire, straw. A few barrels of green wine. You'll be sailing soon. There's a fair wind rising.'

'All aboard!' a woman's voice sang sweetly from The Good Ship Good.

Lily was the first to obey, followed closely by Gus. Then Mordec, who'd stopped to hoist his bookbag onto his shoulder, re-tie his fishing rods together, and nod farewell to the Harbour-Master—a nod that was almost a bow, deepened somehow by the imposing look of the man—began to stride up the gangplank.

'One thing more,' the Harbour-Master said.

Mordec stopped and half turned to look back at him.

'The news brought on the tides these last few days,' the Harbour-Master went on, 'is danger on the western seas, not only storms and strong currents, but also piracy, more plundering, more burning than for many a summer. Please tell Captain Cogg. And tell *her* too, the one who's calling. A fine woman. I think the day is coming near when I'll speak to her myself. But tell them both what I've told you. Tell them that these tidings and opinions come from me.'

'I will,' Mordec promised.

'All aboard!' the voice sang again, and Mordec stepped onto the deck of The Good Ship Good.

The sweet voice belonged, Mordec found, to a slender, white-haired woman, as tall as the Harbour-Master, with a lined yet still beautiful face. Though her hair hung loose as a girl's over her shoulders and down her back, she was at least as old, Mordec thought, as his mother. She stood at the top of the gang-plank to greet the passengers.

'Delfinola, Captain's Mate,' she introduced herself with a friendly nod. 'You'll be giving me your swords and daggers to take faithful care of, if you please.'

Adam had forewarned them that their swords and daggers would be taken away and locked up, and Gus and Mordec were ready to hand theirs over promptly. Lily gave hers up with such obvious reluctance that Delfinola looked at her face with closer attention.

'It's for the safety of all now,' the Mate said. 'You'll be getting them back quick as the flash of a jilter's smile should the need come up at all. And none of you I hope and trust has been so rash as to bring gold or silver on board this darling ship? We are known to carry none, and none will we carry.'

Mordec said he carried only 'a note of credit'—as his grandfather called the letter addressed to a fellow

Lombard in London—and he opened his scrip, the ox-leather pouch strapped to his hip, for Delfinola to see for herself that he spoke the truth. 'See?'

'You do. You speak the truth,' she said, making the word 'truth' sound more like 'troot', so that Mordec needed a moment or two to grasp what she meant.

Yet he had not told the whole truth. Something left untold was that the old man had had a few gold coins sewn into the hem of Mordec's cloak. 'Even the safest ship might be attacked,' Adam had said, 'and if you escape, which of course you would, you might be cast ashore in a strange land and then you would need the gold to survive.'

'But my advice to you is,' the Mate went on, 'never show or tell anyone what is in your scrip. No more than you would tell what is in your heart.'

'Good advice,' Mordec agreed.

'And what do they call you?' Delfinola enquired.

'Mordec son of Hauk.'

'Come then, Mordec son of Hauk. You may stow your bag in here.'

Delfinola opened the doors of a dark cavern under the raised deck in the bows. 'The girls sleep in here when they're not on watch, but they'll not tamper with your things.' ('Wid your tings' was how she said it.) 'And you'll not disturb them.'

'I won't mind if they look. It's mostly books I've got in here,' Mordec told her. He expected her to be surprised, as most people were, to find out that he could read; but if she was, she didn't show it. She said, 'I wouldn't have asked. I'm not of a curious turn of

mind. But is there no armour in there? I was thinking you must have some hidden armour. Anybody
would suppose Vikings would be carrying shields,
helmets. That sort of thing.' ('Ting', she said again,
but by now Mordec was understanding her without
difficulty.) 'But not you? And the other two have
naught but a sword each and a bundle!'

Mordec told her that he and Gus had had armour
made for them more than a year ago, 'when we were
smaller, and we soon grew out of it'.

'We'll have new armour made when we get home.'

Mordec, Gus and Lily were not the only passengers. They watched two more embarking: a thin
monk in a black habit with a portly, cheerful, red-
faced servant who helped him up the gangplank
murmuring encouraging words in a jumble of Italian
and German. Delfinola stretched out a helping
hand. When the monk stood safely on the deck
the servant handed her a sheathed sword, the only
weapon the pair had between them. The black hood
which obscured and shaded the monk's face fell back
while he stood waiting, and revealed heavy-lidded
eyes, sunken blue-stubbly cheeks, and a bony beak
of a nose.

'He looks,' Mordec murmured to Lily, 'Like a bird
of prey.'

'Welcome aboard,' the Mate said as she took the
sword. 'Welcome aboard The Good Ship Good, holy
brother and your good man. I am Delfinola, the
Captain's Mate. Though you'd never suppose it, I am
from Ireland.'

'My name is Forl,' the servant said, smiling back. 'Brother Nico, my master, needs a quiet place to rest.'

'Aye,' Delfinola assured him briskly, 'and we have a place where he may choose, at whim, between the cuddling shelter and the lavish open air.'

The Black Monk himself said nothing at all. When he was settled aft, in the 'lavish open air' near the doors under the raised deck in the stern, Forl returned to the quay to fetch bags and bundles. He was helped by the Harbour-Master to hang them by their straps round his neck and on his shoulders. Forl thanked him heartily, joking with him as if they were old friends.

A little later when Mordec was wandering about the ship, he saw the servant making a soft bed of cushions and furs and setting down a water jug and a white loaf, and heard him talking to his master soothingly. Not a word did the master utter. Forbidding and malign he seemed. His hands, emerging on thin wrists from the wide sleeves of the black habit, were like bird-claws. They felt about and knocked over the water-jug. Fori hurried to refill it from one of the big barrels amidships before he patiently mopped the spill and rearranged the bedding. Later Mordec told Lily and Gus that Brother Nico was very dim-sighted, perhaps blind. 'I guess he's bound for Sam's island,' he added.

'What makes you think that?' Gus said sharply. 'Are you getting second sight, like Sigvard the Skald?'

'As there are Black Monks on Sam's island,' Mordec replied patiently, 'and as we are bound there, it seemed a fair guess—but if you've got a better one, let's hear it.'

Gus looked at Lily to see how she felt about this latest piece of clever talk from Mordec. But Lily only glanced at the monk and the servant without much curiosity. Her thoughts were elsewhere.

'Weigh anchor,' a distant woman's voice commanded, and Delfinola in her dulcet tones repeated the order, calling: 'Weigh an-chor!'

'Loose hawsers,' came next, and Delfinola's echo, 'Loose haw-sers!'

Girls, dressed in the whitest of white tunics and crossbound breeches, scurried about on bare feet to obey.

The Harbour-Master, down on the quayside, raised his hat ceremoniously, bowed to the Captain and again, more profoundly, to Delfinola, and standing there to see them off, began to recede. The fair wind he had promised bulged the sails and carried The Good Ship Good smoothly out of the harbour on to choppier water. She rolled quite a bit but hardly pitched at all.

'Lovely boys, our three young passengers,' the Captain of The Good Ship Good, a stout strong woman, boomed loudly to the Mate, though the two of them stood side by side. Their eyes were fixed on one of the three 'lovely boys' who at that moment was swinging high in the rigging to give a hand with the reefing of a topsail. What with a brisk sea, a blue day, and a sweet breeze blowing, the wide tub of a vessel needed only two sails to keep her rocking westward at a good rate of knots.

The lady-captain's powerful voice carried easily to the six persons poised on the crossbeam of the main-mast, and one of them—the only one not dressed in white—glanced down at the Captain, but was too far away for her amused expression to be caught by the woman who'd spoken. The Captain dropped her voice as she went on to say, 'So handsome and so strong. I hope they don't turn the heads of my more foolish gels. I think it would be best if the gels were told to keep away from them.'

'Yes, it would be a great foolishness if they let their heads be turned by any of those three,' said the Mate in a soft voice which only carried far when she intended it to. 'Especially,' she went on gently, 'if one considers that two of them are Vikings, which, as far as I'm concerned, means that they're prentice murderers, and the third may be that as well, but one thing I can tell you for sure, that one isn't a boy at all, at all.'

'Not a boy?' The Captain turned her soft, full-cheeked, double-chinned face to the Mate's fine-boned one, and her blue, benevolent eyes opened wide to stare into a pair as brown and hard and shiny as fresh-peeled chestnuts. 'What is he then?'

'A girl of course. What else is there?'

'A girl? Which one is a girl? Not that one?' The Captain's surprise made her sound stupid, which she wasn't.

'Yes.'

'But he—she—moves like a boy.'

'She does that.'

'Yet now I come to think of it, he—she—is perhaps rather too pretty to be a boy. And he's—she's—not as brawny as the other two. Lithe, but not brawny. Yes, I see what you mean. But when—how—did you find out?'

'When those three came on board I wondered, had the servants of the Silver Shield told me wrong? Here were three *boys* coming on board when they'd said two boys and a girl. A queen they'd said, to be exact. Two boys and a queen. I was looking forward to the queen, while it was the thought of the boys that was troubling me. Vikings? I said to the men of the Silver Shield, we've never taken Vikings before. I rather think they'll be after cutting our throats and seizing the ship. They're only boys, the Silver Shield men said. And I didn't want to make too much of it. I knew you wouldn't be wanting me to say no when one of them, the Mordec, is connected with their master, your good friend Adam Silvershield himself. Then I needn't ask if he can pay, I said. Full payment has been made in the usual way, said they, and handed me the letters for London.'

'Vikings?' the Captain interrupted. 'Are you sure? There's one of them over there and if I'm not mistaken *he is wearing glasses.*'

'Sure I'm sure. Pay no heed to the glasses. A little civilization settled on them in Italy. And I will say that when they came on board they did not seem bent on murder, neither the Mordec—he's the one who wears the glasses—nor the other whose name is Gus. No. They handed over their weapons without blinking, I can truly say. It was the third one seemed unwilling, the one with the girls now. That's when I looked more closely and saw what it was about him. *He* was not a he at all but a she. Queen Lily she's called.'

'Queen of what? Of where?' the Captain demanded.

'Of the East Fenreach.'

'Then she must be Queen Bertha's daughter. Surely not! Queen Bertha would be too old to have so young a daughter. And anyway, I'm almost certain that she had only one and her name was—what was it? O my memory! Glenda? No—Gloria. So this could be Gloria's daughter. Yes, that's who she is then. The gels can keep company with her, but not with the Vikings, except in the presence of you or me. I wonder what an English queen was doing in Italy? And in the company of Viking boys! There's a story for us to winkle out of them one of these starry nights.'

'And winkle it out we shall, Captain, you may depend upon it!' Delfinola promised, hastily adding, 'Not that I am of a curious turn of mind.'

'Quite so,' the Captain agreed, though she knew perfectly well that Delfinola liked to know as much about everybody as she did herself.

The kindly breeze blew The Good Ship Good on through the balmy day. She continued to roll gently, her hull bulging over the water like a cushion, her prow no more protuberant than the lip of a squat milk-jug on an English breakfast table.

The girls looked at the boys but obeyed orders not to go near them. When Delfinola told them the Captain's order to keep away from the Vikings she reminded them of the punishment for disobedience: a dragging through the sea behind the ship, like bait on a line. None of them had ever been put to this punishment, but they believed Delfinola when she said she would do it with 'a hard heart and a dry eye'.

But it was safe enough to *talk about* the boys among themselves, and some said that Gus was the handsomer of the two and looked more like a warrior; others that Mordec was at least as handsome as Gus although he wore glasses and besides he seemed friendlier. Gus hardly said a word, but they'd heard Mordec talking to Delfinola about tides and winds and storms ahead.

And they watched him fishing over the side of the ship. On the first day he caught two dorados, cooked them himself and added them to the evening meal of bread, salt fish, gull-eggs, wild goose preserved in its own fat, hard cheese, ale and foamy beer, that all sat down to at the same time, except the girls on the watch and Brother Nico and Forl who kept themselves apart.

'And what might you have been doing in Italy, Queen dear, if you don't mind my asking?' the Mate said to Lily when the plates had been taken away and the ale-jugs refilled.

So, as darkness fell and The Good Ship Good sailed on under the stars, the tale was told. The girls sat closely round the Mate in a circle of lantern-light and heard how it happened that Lily, Queen of the East Fenreach, was sailing with two Viking boys from Italy to England. The story came out without much winkling that night, and was told again on the following night to the rest of the crew—and to Forl, who unexpectedly came and sat with them, greeting them affably and contributing a large soft white loaf and a small barrel of beer to the meal.

Mordec told the greater part of it, starting with the dreadful tale of how last year he'd been sentenced to death and was very nearly strangled and drowned in a bog in the Earldom of Linkard, the land next to Lily's queendom, but not, like much of the north of England, ruled by Vikings. Linkard and the Fenreach were allowed their freedom on pain of tribute from the Earl, Mordec explained. He told how he had been arrested there, held prisoner, tried in a court of law, found guilty and condemned for something he had not done, and all because a plot had been laid against him by a fellow Viking boy and a busybody at the Earl's court.

Lily related how she had ridden night and day to fetch Vikings who could help save Mordec.

Gus frowned.

*Would they believe,* Lily asked her audience, *that they wouldn't agree to come to his aid until she promised to show them where gold was buried?*

'Oh!' the girls gasped, some covering their mouths with their hands to show how shocked they were.

'Except Gus,' Lily said.

Gus stopped frowning.

'He came at once. He galloped with me through the night to save his friend.'

'Ah!' the girls sighed, hands dropping from mouths to chests, eyes shifting to Gus.

Gus looked down as he felt his face grow warm.

Lily described how they'd snatched Mordec from the jaws of death at the last moment.

'And so,' she said, 'Mordec promised to help me find my mother, who'd been carried off by a Viking warrior.'

Mordec took up the tale again. He'd sailed home with the Viking fleet. More than a year had passed, when in early spring, he and Gus and two other boys named Hengist and Horsa, journeyed south with traders to reach the island where Lily was waiting for them. Sam's island, he said, the very island they were bound for now.

Then, with Lily, they had gone to Italy, finding their way by Sam's maps. Keeping themselves alive, despite terrible dangers, by using their heads and their swords. At one time Lily had been captured by some travelers who would have taken her back to England, but he and the other boys had found and rescued her.

'With the help of a dancing-girl named Charlotte,' Lily put in.

'With some help from her too,' Mordec agreed.

They went to Mordec's grandfather in the Lombard town of Brevis, and from there to Lily's mother, Queen Gloria, in the city of Nebula.

Lily ended the story by saying briefly that her mother hadn't wanted to return with them, and the other two Vikings were staying on awhile in Brevis, so only three of them—Mordec, Gus and herself—were returning to England.

The friendly Forl exclaimed, 'Bravely done, Queen Lily and Viking lads, bravely done!'

'So you did find your mother but she wouldn't come home with you?' one of the girls asked Lily, hoping to find out why, but Lily didn't want to say much more about it.

'Yes,' she said. 'We found her. She welcomed us of course with feasts and celebration. But she cannot come back to unite the kings and earls and lead an army against the Vikings. She would if she could, but she *cannot*. So she told me to do it.'

Through most of the telling Gus had sat silent. Even when Lily told how he had ridden with her through the night to save Mordec from death in the Earldom of Linkard, and all eyes had turned to look at him and he'd faintly blushed, he had said nothing. He did not smile. The truth was, jealousy had opened in him like hunger, and crumbs of praise from *her* could do little to appease it.

'I wonder,' one girl said in a loud whisper to another, 'why Gus was willing to help Lily find her mother when what she wanted her *for* was to come home and make war on the Vikings?'

Gus spoke then at last, to say gruffly that Vikings couldn't be defeated. But the girls looked at each other and all of them saw that there wasn't one among them who didn't know the truth, that Gus the Viking was in love with Lily the English Queen, and that was why he was so glum.

Next a girl wondered aloud why Mordec had done it, and he answered simply that he owed his life to Lily.

'Does that mean he won't fight against her?' another girl asked the stars.

'No,' Mordec said, thinking how shy the girls must be not to look at him when they spoke to him; 'all Viking men, from the day they turn fifteen, fight in wars.'

The same girl then asked Lily why she had gone to so much trouble to save the life of an enemy.

'Mordec is my friend as well as my enemy,' Lily replied, not noticing how Gus frowned again when she said it. 'And he was unjustly condemned through a wicked trick by another Viking. As I told you, this other boy plotted with a sickening fellow who spends his life messing up other people's lives in the name of doing them good. Master Busybody of Linkard—I call him that to his face. And I'll serve him right. He doesn't know it yet, but I mean to send him to the war in the front of the first attack.'

None of the girls found these answers entirely satisfactory. For them certain questions still hung in the air. They went to bed under the foredeck and dreamt of tall strong yellow-haired boys, and chatted about them in the bright morning as they stood in chest-high barrels filled with brine and, screened by a sail, scrubbed their bare bodies with vegetable-skeletons called 'lufas'.

Some said they were quite sure that Lily had been wrong to save Mordec. If she hadn't, Mordec wouldn't have been honour-bound to help her find her mother, and Gus wouldn't have gone with Mordec and fallen in love with her, and his dreadful sorrow over having to fight to the death with his own true love would never have arisen. Others heartily disagreed.

The discussion was becoming heated when Delfinola put an end to it by summoning them to their defense practice. She or the Captain drilled the girls every day. Swords, daggers, clubs, spiked balls on chains, bows and arrows were handed out. The archers were lined up along the sides of the ship, the rest cut and hammered the air with their weapons until they were breathless. Delfinola was the harder of the two commanders. She had them rushing at sacks of straw uttering blood-curdling cries. 'Don't stop to think,' she shouted. 'Run, roar, stab, slice 'em up, turn, stab again.'

Lily watched, and the idea came to her that she could send the women of England to war as well as the men. And when the girls told her that Captain Anwid was the daughter of the Earl of Felldown, she resolved to persuade Anwid and her father to bring a few thousand men *and women* soldiers into the field against the Vikings.

She talked to the girls about the coming war. They were trained fighters, she said. Would they fight on land?

None of them agreed at once. To them, who'd been taught not only seamanship but also right behaviour by Captain Anwid, a person's loyalty was due to her captain and her people. Only now, when Lily questioned them, did the question arise—who were their people? The idea that the Vikings, who had conquered some of the English lands, were the enemies of *all* the English was a new one to them. They would believe it was true if Captain Anwid said it was. They would fight with Lily if the Captain said they could.

'Ask her then,' Lily urged them. So one of the girls did.

The Captain folded her arms over her bosom and said that if any of them deserted The Good Ship Good to join the army, she personally would trail that gel in the sea until the sharks had eaten every bit of her.

'So the Vikings aren't our enemy too?' the girl asked nervously.

'The Vikings,' Captain Anwid said, 'are everybody's enemy.'

This gave rise to another topic for them to argue over. If the Vikings were their enemy, was it right for them to take Vikings on board as paying passengers? The answer to that came quickly. It must be right, they all agreed, if the Captain did it, because whatever the Captain did was right. Taking Vikings on board your ship, they told each other, was not at all the same as risking your life to save them.

When Lily heard of the Captain's reply, she went to her and asked her directly: 'Will you not bring fighting men and women to join my army?'

The Captain answered with a question of her own. 'It's very important to you to form this army, isn't it?' she said, keeping a steady hand on the rudder and a watchful gaze on the horizon.

'To force the Vikings out of England, yes. Doesn't it matter at all to you?'

'To me personally, no. My recipe for good living,' the Captain said, 'can be given in three words: food, fables, and staying afloat.'

'You could add another word,' Lily said. 'Freedom.'

'The sea is my freedom,' Captain Cogg said in a tone that put an end to the conversation.

Lily was disappointed, and confided as much to Delfinola. The Mate listened sympathetically. But it was the story of Lily and Gus feeling themselves destined to fight each other to the death and yet also to marry each other, that had seized her imagination and continued to thrill her emotions.

'Oh that fate should call one to love where one should hate!' she said to the young Queen.

'You seem to think a lot about love,' Lily said.

'*Think* about it, yes,' Delfinola said. '*Talk* about it, yes. But think and talk about it only. I doubt I'll go in for it ever again.'

'Why not?' Lily enquired.

'I lost both my loves,' Delfinola said sadly.

'Lost them? How?'

'They went to war,' the Mate said. 'Two prince-lings. Each in turn came courting me. Each left me a castle when he was cut down in battle.'

'You own two castles?' Lily said. 'Where?'

'In Ireland,' said Delfinola. 'Delapidated things, stony cold.'

'Do you live in them?'

'I do not live on dry land at all. What should I do after I lost my second love but give myself to the desolate sea?' she asked mournfully, looking at the sparkling water under a cloudless sky. 'Twice to have loved and lost! And each time, Oh it went so deep! Into the marrowbone. And now I'm growing old. Tell me—do you not despise my withered face? Look at it. D'you see? None will ever clamor for me again. None but the wild waves with their terrible hunger.'

'My grandmother, Queen Bertha, is older than you, and she's still beautiful. You are too, though you're not like her. Lots of men admire her, I happen to know. And you—what about the Harbour-Master at Genova? I heard Mordec telling you what he said. He wants you to know that he admires you.'

'Ah,' sighed Delfinola, 'yes. I have been told about him before now. Many a message I've had from him. A handsome man, I can see that. And good, I've been told. And he has a grand house above the harbour. And regular fees coming in from his share of harbour dues. And no known enemies to plot his downfall. I have enquired about him, you see.'

'Well then?' Lily said, a little impatiently. 'He's not exactly a prince, but his house in Genova would be warmer than a castle in Ireland, I should think.'

Delfinola shook her head. 'The heart grows old,' she said. 'And what a person needs changes from age to age. If there is a man for me yet, I'll know him when I meet him.'

# the blind messenger

On they sailed through cloudless days and starry nights. Each bright morning fish of many colours could be seen streaking through the clear water. Dorados with their visible teeth came swimming alongside. Gus, balancing himself on crates and barrels, took aim and hurled a harpoon—lent to him by Delfinola—down into the blue-green water, his eye judging the speed and path of the creature to hit it with deadly accuracy; yet he missed. Over and over again he hauled in the dripping harpoon with never a thing on the end of it. And then Mordec would come along with a whole pailful of fish he'd caught with a hook-and-line; not all good for eating, but among them a dorado or two and perhaps a young tunny. Gus told himself that there was a good deal more satisfaction to be got by fighting with a fish to conquer it than by luring it with a scrap of rat on a drifting string.

The nights were quiet and peaceful. The ship rocked soothingly. Gus was wakeful and sat up for much of the night watching, from a vantage point on top of a pile of bales, Lily asleep in one place, Mordec in another.

One night Delfinola sang them a song she had made up. She stood gazing out over the dark sea, a breeze stirring her white hair, and sang sweetly and sadly:

*She cried out 'We will never part,'*
*And shot two arrows in his heart,*
*One named Love, the other Death.*
*He plunged his sword into her side*
*'I have no choice, my lovely bride,'*
*And one last slow and painful breath*
*They shared—then lips to lips they died.*

Some of the girls sobbed. Gus looked for Lily, but she was nowhere to be seen. Then he looked for Mordec, and saw him sitting a little apart, looking at the stars.

Later that night Gus saw a lantern being brought close to the covered figure of the Black Monk who lay near the doors under the raised deck aft which the ship's company called the 'poopdeck'. The hand that held it belonged to Forl, as Gus could see when the man bent his face close to his master's.

What Gus could not see was Forl's other hand groping in the monk's scrip and finding a parchment there; a parchment of the finest, lightest quality; not rolled but folded flat. Nor did he see that Forl very carefully drew it out and put another, just as fine and light, in its place.

In any case what Forl was doing was of no interest to Gus. What could it matter to him if the man fussed over his master? Gus gathered his cloak closer about his hunched shoulders, for the breeze had freshened, and he turned back to watch the bundles on the deck, one here and one over there, which he knew to be Lily and Mordec.

Then his eye was caught again by the moving lantern. This time Forl carried it some distance from his master's sleeping form and set it down on a crate. In its light he unfolded something and peered closely at it for a moment. Then he looked furtively about him—but not upward where he would have seen Gus's dark form against the stars—and went softly to the ship's side. He held up the thing and let it flutter for a moment in the wind before letting it go. The wind whisked it off. He didn't look to see where to. He put out his lantern and crept away to his own bed.

And Gus would never have known what it was that Forl had thrown to the wind, if it hadn't blown into his face.

'What the—?' he muttered, pulling off the thing that had come abruptly out of nowhere and plastered itself against his eyes, nose and mouth. He was about to throw it aside and let it sail on over his shoulder when, in the dimness of the starlight, he made out that there was writing on it.

Now curiosity stirred his thoughts. Regretting for once that he couldn't read, he folded the parchment in its creases and tucked it under his belt. He'd get Mordec to read it to him in the morning.

'I can read it all right,' Mordec whispered as he and Gus and Lily, huddled in a narrow passage between bales and crates to which Gus had led them after breakfast, pored over the parchment. 'But I can't tell you what it means. I could puzzle it out a bit, I think, if it was Italian. But it isn't, you see. It's Latin.'

'And you're sure it's addressed to the Abbot?' Lily said. 'Yes. And Gus thinks Forl stole it from Brother Nico.'

'I know he did. He was bending over him and then he went to the side of the ship and tried to get rid of it and it blew straight in my face.'

'But how do we know it's from the Pope?'

'It's got the Pope's seal on it,' Mordec said, pointing to a small disc of red wax with a pair of crossed keys in it. 'I'm pretty sure that's what it is. So whoever wrote it could get at the Pope's seal. Or forge it.'

'But why do you think it says something about Sam?'

'I can see the name Gaudinus. I guess that's the Latin for Gaudin—Sam's name, and his grandmother's.'

'So,' said Gus, 'it's telling the Abbot of the Black Monks on the island to give some message to Sam and his grandmother.'

'Or do something bad to them. Remember that the Abbot is no friend to Sam.'

'Hates him,' Lily said. 'But he had a high opinion of Horsa. You remember he wanted Horsa to stay and join his abbey?' She and Mordec looked at each other and laughed. Gus said, 'I don't see what's funny about that. He just happened to like Horsa.'

Neither Lily nor Mordec cared to explain to him that the Abbot hadn't asked Horsa to stay because he *liked* him, but because he wanted him to become a Christian and fight for the Church.

'We must try to find out exactly what this Latin means,' Mordec said.

'Maybe,' Lily said, 'the Captain or Delfinola can understand Latin.'

'We'll ask,' Mordec said.

Later, giving no reason, Mordec did ask Delfinola whether she or the Captain or any of the girls knew Latin, and Delfinola, without wondering why he asked, replied that none of them did.

'But Brother Nico now. Sure he'd be able to help you.'

Well then,' Lily said, 'let's ask him.'

'But what if Forl tried to throw it away so that whatever the order was wouldn't be carried out? Forl must know what it says and he must be trying to stop it reaching the Abbot. Forl could be trying to save Sam—don't you see?' Gus felt proud of his reasoning. He would show Lily that Mordec wasn't the only Viking who could reason well.

'Or maybe,' Mordec said, 'someone else told him to steal it and destroy it.'

'Someone else? But he's loyal to his master!' Gus exclaimed.

'Or seems to be,' Mordec said.

'You mean,' said Lily, 'he makes himself out to be such a good servant because he's really a traitor in the pay of someone else?'

'It's possible. Remember what my grandfather told us about Rome. Everyone fighting everyone.'

Gus stood up. 'Come on. If Brother Nico's the only person who can tell us what it says, let's ask him. Then we can decide what to do next.'

'He won't tell us,' Lily said. 'He'll make us give it back to him, and he'll give it to the Abbot, and if it is an order to do some harm to Sam we'll have lost our chance to stop it.'

'But Brother Nico must know what orders he's carrying anyway,' Gus said.

'I suppose so,' Lily said. 'But—maybe they have to come in writing, like treaties, which have to be written down.'

'Perhaps it would be best to wait and give it to Sam,' Mordec said. 'Unless—'

'Unless what?'

'What if it orders the Abbot to *stop* being cruel to Sam and his grandmother? If we give it to Sam and Sam finds that *that* is what it says—'

'Then he can give it to the Abbot.'

'But if *he* gives it to the Abbot, won't the Abbot say that Sam must have written it?'

'But it's got the Pope's seal on it.'

'Yes, but—The Abbot might say that Sam did that by magic. Don't forget what the Abbot says about Sam—that he's a magician doing things the Church doesn't like. No—we must try to find out what it says before we reach Sam's island.'

'But how?' Gus and Lily looked at Mordec, expecting him to think of a way.

Mordec gazed out to sea as though trying to read the answer on the water or the sky. At last he said, 'I think I have an idea.' He crawled into the dark cavern under the foredeck where his bag was stowed and came out with a book in his hand.

'Wait here,' he said to Gus and Lily.

He found Forl amidships, preparing his master's breakfast, stirring a yellowish porridge over a low flame in the iron bucket which did for a kitchen range.

'Good morning,' Mordec said politely.

'Ah, one of my young Viking friends,' Forl answered. He put down the ladle, held out a hand and clasped Mordec's for a moment, saying, 'A very good morning to you too.'

Mordec thought, 'You clasp someone's hand who seems to be friendly, but it could be the hand of a forger, or even your own killer.'

'Had your breakfast?' Forl enquired, returning to work with the ladle. 'Or will you share my polenta with me? I'll serve my master first and then we two can sit down together.'

'Thank you but I've eaten. I came to ask you if you could help me understand some lines in this book—'

'Ah, sorry, my good friend, but I can't read. You can read?'

'A little.'

'You're lucky. Who taught you?'

'My mother. But there are lots of things I still want to learn. I've learnt very little Italian. And no Latin. D'you know Latin?'

'Only what we repeat in church. Is it Latin you have there?'

'In part, yes, I think so.'

'Then you should read it to my master. He will tell you what it means. He knows every language in the world. But he can't read because he can't see. Read it to him when he's finished his breakfast and he'll tell you what it means.'

'You think he would?'

'He would. My master is the kindest, most just and loving man on God's earth. I'm blest to have such a master.'

'He's kind?' Mordec exclaimed before he could stop himself. 'He doesn't look it!'

'He looks troubled because he has no strength and he cannot see. But if you only knew him, you'd know I speak the truth.'

Fine, Mordec thought, but now the problem was how to talk to the monk without the servant being there too.

'Come with me, my friend,' Forl said, 'and we'll tell him what you're after.'

Brother Nico sat waiting in his solitary corner, his face lifted to the sun, his eyes closed. Forl spoke softly to him, put bowl and spoon in his hands, and went on, 'I have one of the Viking lads with me, Master. His name is Mordec son of Hauk. He has something written in Latin that he wants to read to you. He can read. Isn't that wonderful, Master? He is a Viking and yet he can read! But he has no Latin, and he wants to know what it means.'

'Is it—Holy Scripture?' Brother Nico asked in a voice almost drowned by breath, every word grating in his throat. 'I will not—put Holy Writ into any—other language.'

'No no, it's not,' Mordec said hurriedly.

'Then return in—the late afternoon—when the sun is low—and the shadow of the sail—lies on this—part—of the ship—and we may feel—cool enough to—put our minds—to work.'

'He will let me talk to him in the early evening,' Mordec told Gus and Lily. 'If necessary I'll just ask him to send Forl away.'

'But what will you say? How will you get him to tell you what the letter says?'

'I don't know. I'll think of a way when the time comes.'

Meanwhile there was nothing for him to do but eat, doze, read and fish. He'd settled down with a book when to his surprise Lily asked him if he'd teach her to read.

'I will,' he said.

She sat beside him.

'I've been thinking,' she said, 'about my mother. I can't blame her really for not wanting to come back to our land. If it wasn't for the Earl's court over the river, we'd be no better than savages. My grandmother calls me a savage. She can't read either, but she knows a lot. She often said to me, "You're a queen yet you're not a lady like Jessica who's only an earl's daughter".'

'You once told me that Jessica offered to teach you to read.'

'She did. But I used to think that if I spent time reading and writing I'd stop being good at hunting and fighting. I thought learning from books would make me soft. But I know better now. What I've been thinking is, reading and writing might help me get the lords and kings of England to join together in war.'

'So—if I teach you to read, I'll be giving you more help to make war on us?' Mordec said, laughing.

'Yes,' Lily said simply, and laughed too.

Gus, leaning over the side with his harpoon raised, heard their laughter, and his jealousy felt hotter than the sun.

'Here's the heathen boy come with his Latin,' Forl told Brother Nico. 'Mordec son of Hauk.'

Brother Nico had heard the approaching footsteps. 'Leave us Forl.'

It was as simple as that! Forl was dismissed and Mordec was left alone with the monk.

Brother Nico waited, listening until he was sure that Forl had walked out of earshot, then he said in a kindly enough tone, 'Do you—trust your—fellow men, Mordec son of Hauk?'

Mordec had good reason to say no, but—'Some,' he replied.

'Your—fellow—Vikings, I suppose?'

'Not all.'

'Do they—trust you?'

'I've given them no reason not to.'

'Why do you—trust me?'

The question took Mordec by surprise. He hesitated.

'You want me—to translate—Latin—into your own—language. Why do you—assume that I'll—give you the true meaning?'

'Why wouldn't you?'

'If the book is—a blasphemous work—against the Church and its teachings, I would—think it right to—keep the meaning from you and—teach you something else instead.'

'It isn't a book,' Mordec confessed, deciding to come straight to the point. 'It's a letter.'

'A letter? Whose? From whom and—to whom?'

'I don't know.'

'How did you—come by it?'

'I—I found it.'

'Where?'

'Here, on the ship.'

'And it's written in Latin?'

'I believe so.'

'You know no Latin at all?'

'A few words only.'

'Such as?'

'*Gaudium longum non est.* I know that because it's on walls in the town of Brevis where my grandfather lives.'

'The Lombard town. I—know—the town and I know it is their motto. Do you know—what the motto means?'

'It means you can't be happy all the time.'

'On earth,' the monk said. 'They should add—on earth.'

'They don't,' Mordec said.

'Right. They're—blasphemers, those—Lombards, if not—completely—Godless. Fit—friends for heathens.' There was no hate or anger in the way he said the condemning words. 'But I—understand—that you can read?'

'Yes.'

'Try the Latin. You'll—pronounce it—wrongly—like the barbarian—you are.' He did not smile as he said that, but his tone remained gentle. Perhaps, Mordec thought, he simply lacked the breath to rage or fume. 'But—I'll know what—you're saying. Begin.'

For good or ill, Mordec felt he was committed now to this risky endeavour. He unfolded the fine parchment, read the first few words aloud and stopped, expecting the monk to translate bit by bit.

'Don't stop. Read all of it.'

Mordec stumbled his way through the letter. When he'd finished the monk was silent. Mordec looked at the sightless eyes.

'What does it mean?' he asked.

'You found this letter? Where—exactly?'

'The wind blew it into my friend's face.'

'So the wind was carrying it?—It might have been blown—from anywhere? From some—other ship? Or—even—from the land?'

'I don't think so.'

'And what makes you not think so?'

'I made out the name of Abbot Alonso de Llama. I think it's the same Abbot Alonso de Llama that I saw and spoke to when I was on the island we're bound for. We stopped there on the way to Italy, in the castle of the Gaudins.'

'Which shares the island—with the abbey. And they are—your friends, these—Gaudins. Very well. I'll tell you—what the letter says. It instructs—the Abbot to—make peace with them. To leave them—in safe possession—of their lands—and castles, farms—villages—slaves and all. It—instructs him—not to make an enemy of the man known as—Sam of the West or—any—of the great landowners—of France.'

'That's good—very good!' Mordec exclaimed. 'Here—the letter is yours. Take it, give it to the Abbot—'

'I? You think this letter was—entrusted to me—and that I—lost it?'

'Yes. I mean—aren't you on a mission to the Abbot?'

'I am.'

'Only to speak to him? Not to take him any written message? You weren't carrying a letter to him?'

'On the contrary. Precisely to take him—a written message. A—letter, as you say.'

'But not this letter?'

'Truly I have no idea—what the message is—in the letter I must give him. I was not told. And they send me—because—I am too blind—to read it. The servant—they let me take with me—cannot read at all. Only the Abbot—must know his instructions.'

'But you ordered me to read it to you.'

'To read *that* letter, yes. And it brings up—many questions. Such as—who are you? What harm are you plotting? But—I must leave—investigation—to the Abbot.'

'This letter can't do harm!' Mordec protested.

'If these Gaudins—are dangerous to the Church—then such orders as those—would be misdirections.'

Mordec thought for a moment, then he said: 'Let me ask you this. Did you have a letter, and is it now missing?'

'I had a letter and it is not—missing. I have it still. If I didn't—that one could be mine, and I would—not have asked you—to read it to me. But—the letter entrusted to me is—still in my scrip. I seek it—often—with my fingers. I find it there now.'

'And you had only one?'

'Only one. Now we'll say no more—about this—you and I. Until we get—to the island. Give me the letter you are holding. Put it—in my hand. Leave it with me.'

'What will you do with it?'

'It can only—cause—confusion.'

'You want to destroy it?'

The monk made no answer, but continued to hold out his hand.

Mordec rose, folded the letter, put it in his scrip and walked away. He half expected the monk to call him back, but neither the monk nor Forl said another word about the letter on that day or any other as long as the voyage lasted.

As they sailed on under fair skies, Mordec was troubled by the idea that The Good Ship Good was bearing some danger to Sam and his grandmother.

The mysterious menace loomed like a bank of storm clouds on an horizon.

# the red and the black

The Good Ship Good came to a safe mooring in the mainland harbour opposite the little island where Sam of the West lived with his grandmother, and Abbot Alonso de Llama ruled over his monks.

Mordec, Gus and Lily, with Captain Anwid, Delfinola, Brother Nico and his servant Forl, sailed to the island in two of the pretty white boats with rose-coloured sails which Sam and his grandmother Djil kept for to-ing and fro-ing, and which the monks of the abbey also made free use of. The old man at the oars greeted them in German, and understood Mordec when he inquired what had become of the boy Arnulf who had been oarsman when last they were here.

'Gone to join the Army of the Redeemed,' the old man replied. 'A troop of brigands,' he growled, and spat over the side of the boat. 'The Pope don't know what he's doing giving arms to young savages like that and sending them off killing and marauding.'

'It seems to me that a man is made Pope,' Mordec said, 'because he does things that no one else can understand.'

On the landing stage stood the Abbot himself, waiting to greet Brother Nico. The two Black Monks bowed solemnly to each other. Then, seated in golden chairs, they were borne by six monks each, the Abbot first, up the steep and narrow mountain path to the abbey. Forl traipsed after them with Brother Nico's baggage. Mordec watched them go until they were swallowed by the dark in the abbey's cavernous portal. Then he followed the others along the branching path which led to the Gaudins open gates.

And here he was again in the bright hall, and mounting the curving stairs, and now entering the big round room which looked out over the sea. And here were Sam and his grandmother Djil and their three greyhounds. As always, Sam was dressed in the red garments which, along with his red hair and a reputation for possessing extraordinary powers, earned him his name, 'The Red Magician'.

The welcome was warm. 'We've been expecting Anwid and Delfinola any day now,' Djil said, 'but your arrival with them, Mordec and Gus and Queen Lily, is a happy surprise.'

The greyhounds seemed glad to see them too, sitting up and panting. One of them came to Mordec when he was seated, lifted a heavy paw and dropped it on his knee.

Hung on the wall were tapestries woven by Djil, in which she recorded events of their house and times. She showed them one depicting Mordec, Gus and Lily arriving in this very room on their way to find Lily's mother, and being greeted by Sam, Djil, and the greyhounds; and another in which Captain Anwid and Delfinola sat at a table playing a board-game with Djil while Sam stood at a window gazing out to sea through a long tube.

A welcoming feast was soon spread, and Mordec, after the plain fare of the ship, devoured it first with his eyes. He felt suddenly how much he had missed fine food since leaving his grandfather's house, and here were flagons of night-red wine, bowlsful of berries and cherries, striped apples, black plums, seven heaps of honeyed loaves, cucurbs and their yellow flowers frosted with sugar-of-beet, a brown roasted goose, and another, and a giant carp on colewort, its amber scales glistering with oil of nuts.

As they feasted, Sam told Mordec and Gus news of the wars in Italy. The Army of the Redeemed had attacked and massacred non-Christians in the north of Italy, but many of the young adventurers had themselves been slaughtered when they'd clashed with Vikings. So Sam had recently been informed, and he assured Mordec that the town of Brevis was not listed among those which had been invaded.

Two hours later they were still at the table, the Captain and Mordec answering innumerable questions put to them by Sam. He wanted their news of the seas and the ports, of the weather, trade, what they had seen of war in Italy, what the Lombards were saying about the fighting factions and other matters, and what the merchants and the priests were doing. And he needed to know how good his maps had proved to be.

So they had they found Lily's mother? Why then was she not returning home with Lily? Or Hengist

and Horsa with Mordec and Gus? He was special-
ly pleased to hear that they had put to use a lesson
he had taught them so effectively that it may have
helped them win a battle: how to move the last object
in a long row by striking the first against the second,
so sending a force through all of them without moving the ones in between.

At last Djil interrupted to say that she and Anwid
and Delfinola would have the table cleared so that they
could settle down to a game of Eyes and Nose.

Mordec watched them play. It was a gambling game.
Each player spun a golden arrow balanced on a pin
in the middle of a round polished wooden board on
which the numbers 1 to 6 were painted in gold. On another larger board a road was painted, and divided into
sections numbered 1 to 100. The section numbered
100 had a nose painted on it, with an empty eye on
either side. Each lady had chosen two matching jewels—two blue, two red, two green, or two white—to
move forward along the road, from one to six sections
at a time according to the number the arrow came to
rest on. She could move only one of her two jewels
in each of her goes, but which was her own choice.
She had to be the first to get both her jewels into the
eyes to win the game, and the winner took whatever
the other had staked before the game began. No one,
Mordec noticed, actually handed over gold or silver.
Instead the players exchanged little ivory sticks with
sums of money written on them. 'They're credit notes
of a kind,' Anwid explained to him. 'Now and then
we add them up to see who's won the most.'

'Will you ever pay what you owe?' he asked.

'No need,' the ladies chorused.

A servant came in and murmured a message in Sam's ear.

'The Abbot,' Sam said aloud, 'to see me?'

At once the room which had been full of mirth and chatter became silent and all turned to the door as the Abbot entered, holding his hands pressed together on his chest in the posture of prayer. His hood was laid back, so when he bowed he gave them a glimpse of his pink scalp circled by fair curls.

He advanced into the room on quick short steps. Four monks followed him, hooded so that their faces were all but invisible. Sam rose.

'I have come to summon you to trial,' the Abbot said quietly. 'You see that I have come myself, in person.' And he bowed again.

'Good of you,' Sam said. 'But for what am I to be tried? And on whose authority?' He looked steadily at the Abbot, and Mordec thought his eyes showed amusement rather than fear.

'A letter has come from Rome,' the Abbot replied, solemnly, though his cherry-red lips curved into a smile as he went on in his quiet tones: 'The highest of Church authorities orders me to try you for practicing sorcery and the black arts, and acquiring blasphemous knowledge with the help of the Devil.'

'Who has falsely reported to Rome that I do such things?' Sam enquired.

'I sent word, as was my duty, that you predict storms, heal the sick, examine the insides of vegetables and beasts, watch sea-fowl, gather stones, and seem wise beyond the usual limits of mortal men. Rome would have me find out if you do these things in the service of the Devil.'

'Thank you,' Sam said, 'for thinking me wise.'

Djil rose and advanced towards the Abbot. 'You're not taking him away, Alonso? You won't be locking him up?'

'Locking him up!' Captain Anwid exclaimed, and she and Delfinola came to stand on either side of Sam like a pair of guards; which prompted Mordec, after only a moment's hesitation in which he wondered if a heathen's support might do Sam more harm than good in the Abbot's eyes, to step forward too and stand beside the Captain. Gus and Lily joined him. 'Let the Abbot see,' Mordec thought, 'that Sam has fearless friends!'

'*How* you will be tried has been left to me to decide,' the Abbot said, keeping his eyes on Sam alone. 'I'll let you know tomorrow what form the trial will take. Meanwhile, do not leave the island.' He looked round at the others. 'None of you may leave it. I have sent all the boats to the mainland and set guards on both shores.'

'You *what?*' Captain Anwid exploded, following the words with a sound that was halfway between a laugh and a bark. 'Don't make me laugh, sir! I can whistle a boat over here with my gels at the oars any time I choose.'

The Abbot fixed his gaze on her and said coldly, 'And then I shall have to take him away and lock him up.' Upon which Anwid felt Djil's hand lightly touch her own, and she let the matter drop. 'I shall also be enquiring into the activities of your younger guests,' the Abbot went on, now looking at Mordec. 'I think they know why.'

Mordec and Gus both folded their arms, lifted their chins and glared at the Abbot defiantly. The Abbot bowed again and left the room, followed by his four faceless monks.

Sam said to the greyhounds, 'No runs on the mainland for you three for the next few days.' They hung their heads and licked his hands as though to console him for their loss, but cheerfully followed their master and his friends to his watch-room at the top of the tower.

When its door was shut, Mordec asked Sam: 'Can they spy on us here? Could the Abbot's men hear what we're saying?'

Sam shook his head.

'Good. We have something to tell you about the letter the Abbot got from Rome. It wasn't the *real* letter.'

'Not the real letter? Explain what you mean.'

Gus said, 'The messenger from Rome is a monk named Brother Nico. He sailed with us on The Good Ship Good, and when we were at sea his servant Forl stole the real letter while the monk was asleep and put another one in his scrip.'

'How do you know?'

'Forl tried to throw the real letter away and the wind blew it in my face,' Gus said.

'So you have it?'

'I have it,' Mordec said, handing it to Sam.

'You've read it?' Sam asked.

'Mordec couldn't read much of it because it's in Latin,' Lily said, 'but even then he managed to make out that it's about you and your grandmother.'

Gus's lips tightened. Why, he thought, did she have to praise Mordec even when he *couldn't* do something?

'So—' Sam went on with his questions to Mordec, 'you don't know what it says?'

'Yes, we do,' Mordec said. 'Or at least we think we do—if it says that the Abbot mustn't do anything bad to you or any of the French landowners. Is that what it says?'

'In effect, yes. How did you find out?'

'I read it to Brother Nico. He couldn't read it himself because he's blind, but he told me what it meant because he said it was some trick I was trying to play on him, and if he'd thought it was the real letter he wouldn't have told me.'

'He didn't believe that Forl had stolen it,' Gus said.

'He simply didn't believe it? Didn't even wonder if it might be true?'

Mordec, Gus and Lily shook their heads.

'He could feel a letter in his scrip and he said he knew it was the very same one he'd been carrying all the time,' Mordec said.

'He seemed to think that *Mordec* was trying to trick him into delivering the wrong letter,' Lily said indignantly. 'But why would Mordec want to do that? *We* didn't know he was coming to your island to bring a message from Rome about you,' Lily said.

'So that's what the Abbot meant when he said he'd be "enquiring into your activities",' Sam said.

'Will you take this letter to the Abbot?' Gus wanted to know.

'Let me think,' Sam murmured, and after a moment or two revealed his thoughts. 'We know Brother Nico has told him about it, which means that the Abbot will be suspicious of it. On the other hand the Abbot has met you before and he can't easily believe that you're involved with some faction in Rome. I think he'll have to consider the possibility that this is the real letter. So—yes, you must show it to him.'

'Who—me?' Mordec asked. 'Wouldn't he believe you sooner than me? He thinks of all Vikings as heathens who have no sense of honour and don't know truth from lies.'

'He thinks worse of me,' Sam said. 'You take it to him. You and Gus and Lily. Tell him how you came by it, Gus. And you, Mordec, how you only know what's in it because Brother Nico told you. He won't be pleased with it, but he'll have to take it into account when he thinks about what to do with me. But first I shall make a copy of it, and Mordec and Anwid and Delfinola will sign a declaration that it is a true copy.'

'And show the copy to the Abbot?' Mordec said. 'And keep this one?'

Sam shook his head. 'He'll have to see the one you and Gus found. I'll keep the copy.'

The Abbot received them in his office, seated behind a polished table on a tall-backed chair. Four monks stood ready to do his bidding.

'I was expecting you,' he said, fixing his gaze on Mordec. 'Brother Nico told me what passed between him and you, and warned me that you'd be coming to me with a story about a letter. Tell it to me. I'm listening.'

He heard them out, first Gus telling how the letter blew in his face, then Mordec how Brother Nico had told him what it was about.

When they were finished, the Abbot reached a hand out across the table, and Mordec, after a moment's hesitation, put the letter in it.

The Abbot read it several times, then suddenly looked up and barked a command at the attendant monks: 'Seize them, The boys. Only the boys.'

'No, no!' Lily protested. 'What do you mean to do with them?'

'Stand aside, my lady,' the Abbot said firmly. 'No hands will be laid on you. As an English queen you will be treated with respect—unless we find out that there is a plot against us in England and that you are taking part in it.'

'I want to know what you'll do to them,' Lily insisted, not budging an inch, and keeping a hand on each Viking's shoulder.

'Search them,' the Abbot said, simultaneously answering Lily and getting the obedient monks moving again.

Lily didn't try to prevent the search. She reminded herself that there was nothing incriminating to be found on either of them.

'Here, Father, look at these,' one of the monks called out; triumphantly, holding up some hareskins which he'd pulled from Gus's boots.

Again the Abbot held out his hand, 'Letters,' he said, inspecting the writing. 'Of a rough kind,' he added.

He read every word, studied the drawings, then turned his violet-blue eyes on Gus again.

'So it is true that you Vikings are in alliance with the Lombards and—these tell me—giving them military aid?' he asked.

'Two Vikings are,' Gus said. 'The two who sent the letters with us.'

'And what were *you* doing in the Lombard town of Gaudium Brevis?'

Mordec spoke up. 'My grandfather is a Lombard, and I was visiting him.'

'Hmm.' The Abbot read the letters again, re-examined the drawings, and handed them all back to Gus, asking, 'What is your connection with the Gaudins?'

Gus finished tucking the hareskins back into his boots, folded his arms, tipped his head back and tightened his lips to indicate that he would say no more.

But Mordec, seeing no reason why the Abbot's last question shouldn't be answered, said, 'Don't you remember us? We came here for the first time in the spring, to meet Queen Lily and go with her to Italy to find her mother.'

'I remember you well,' the Abbot said. 'But I know so little of you and your purposes, and have so much cause from knowledge and experience to mistrust Vikings, that our merely having met before does not save you from my suspicions.'

'You won't destroy the letter—the one we brought you—will you?' Mordec asked him, his own voice loaded with suspicion.

'I'll think about it,' the Abbot said. He leant his forearms on the table, each tucked into the sleeve of the other, and stared hard at Mordec for half a minute or more, and at Gus for even longer. Then he said, 'It is no use, you know, defying the will of God.'

This provoked Gus into speaking again. 'It's no use defying any god,' he said sharply. 'Thor is my protector. If you harm me, beware of his hammer.'

'Sad heathen nonsense!' the Abbot said, shaking his head in pity and exasperation. 'Go—but I warn you again, do not try to leave the island.'

# the abbot's prayer

Sam slept well that night, but the Abbot did not.

All through the hours of darkness he paced about his office. One candle burned on his table. Its wavering light fell on the two letters which lay side by side. Every now and then he stopped and examined them.

Try as he might, he could not tell from the writing or the seal which was the one he ought to obey. But one instructed him to put Sam of the West on trial for sorcery and practicing the Black Arts, and to execute him and seize all his property for the Church if he was found guilty; while the other ordered him to treat Sam with all courtesy, to believe nothing said against him, and to promise him peaceful possession of all that he owned. Both told him to obey immediately.

There was no time to send a deputation to Rome to find out from the Pope himself which orders were the right ones.

The Vikings stuck to their story about how they'd found the letter. Could they have made it up, he wondered again and again, to protect the Gaudins? But if so, how did they do it, how did they forge the Pope's seal, and how did they find out about the other letter in the first place? One of them could read and write, but knew no Latin, and would surely not have dared to rummage in Brother Nico's scrip?

Had everything been prepared by others before the voyage, and the Vikings merely put to use as the instruments of another's plot? If so, what was the part of the Lombards in it? Were the Vikings themselves conspiring with factions in Rome, with or without the Lombards? There was no way of knowing. They were heathens of course, so not to be trusted—any more than an English queen who dressed like a boy to deceive the whole world. But to try and extract confessions from them by force could bring the fury of the Northmen down upon the abbey, France, even Rome and the Pope himself.

'High time the Vikings were turned into Christians!' the Abbot murmured to himself. 'We must send missionaries to them. And if they don't succeed soon enough, we must send the Army of the Redeemed against them again, this time in England, under my own command.'

But such resolutions did not help him with his present difficulty.

The Abbot had respectfully questioned Brother Nico too. At first the blind monk insisted that the story the Vikings told couldn't be true. At last he admitted it was possible that a letter had been taken from his scrip while he slept and another, a forgery, put in its place. But he was certain his faithful servant Forl would never do such a thing.

Still, the Abbot had questioned Forl, who'd wept like a child at the very idea that anyone thought he might play a trick on his beloved master. Why, he'd give his own life to save him! The Vikings were lying. That's how they repaid him for his friendship! He wished them no harm, he wished no one any harm, but it was too bad of them to make up such lies. Anyone who knew him would tell the Abbot what an obedient and loving servant he was to Brother Nico. Did the Abbot take the word of heathens above his?

So the Abbot paced and pondered.

'If I do *this*, then *that* might happen. Dangerous. If I do *that*, then *this* might happen. Also dangerous.'

The night was paling, stars setting, and a cool wind stirring over the sea when he came to his first decision: he would hold a trial, and hope to find out the truth. If he found Sam guilty with good reason, then surely no one in Rome would want a sorcerer left alive to carry on with his wicked ways. If he found him not guilty, no one could say he, Alonso da Llama, had failed in his duty.

He felt calmer, and for a few moments lay down on his iron cot, sinking into the goose-feather bed which was spread on top of it.

But soon he was up and pacing again.

What form should the trial take? To ask questions and hear answers seemed to him a perfectly useless way of finding out the truth. Most people didn't listen; or if they listened, they couldn't answer; or if they answered, they didn't make sense; or if they made sense, they were probably lying. But, he told himself, Sam *would* listen, and answer, and make sense. And probably tell the truth. But how to be sure? What questions could he ask which would reveal the indisputable truth?

Pacing and pacing, he began to devise them. But to every good question the Abbot could think of he could also think of a good answer, and he was sure that Sam would think of it too. Sam was clever. He could make people believe him.

And the people liked him and would be on his side if he disputed with the Abbot in a court of law. So the trial of Sam should not take place publicly where anyone who wanted to could watch and listen, but privately. A few witnesses must be present of course, but they could be monks, trained to keep silent.

'Then,' the Abbot thought, 'I would say—*this*. But Sam would say—*that*. So why do I need to have him up before me to say what I already know he'll say?'

The Abbot prayed for guidance, but still the words slid back and forth between him and the Sam of his imagination; until light broke over the sea—and broke within him too. He had a strange and marvelous idea. And while he could never say how he arrived at it, and so believed it was sent to him in answer to his prayers, he was perfectly sure that it was right, good, and beautiful.

He and Sam would argue *without a word being spoken by either of them*. The trial would be held in silence.

# the abbot demands the impossible

It was late morning before Sam was fetched by two hooded monks to hear from the Abbot himself how his trial was to be conducted. He soon returned.

'What does he say? What will he do?' Djil asked as soon as he walked in. 'What sort of trial is it to be?'

'We'll save you!' Anwid said, without waiting to hear his answer.

'It's a terrible thing when the Church itself does the work of the Devil!' Delfinola crooned sorrowfully.

The Vikings and Lily waited. Sam told his grandmother, 'No sort of trial that anyone's ever heard of before. We are to argue with each other.'

'Argue?'

'That's what he's decided. We argue directly with each other, he and I.'

'What about?' Mordec asked.

'He didn't say.'

'What do you suppose?' Djil asked.

'What do *you* suppose, Grandmother?'

Djil shook her head. 'Creation? Man's place in it? The nature of sin? Whatever abbots worry about. But what else did he say will happen?'

'If I win the argument,' Sam said, 'we shall be left free and we'll keep all our property. If I lose, I'll be thrown from the tower, and the Church will seize all that we own.'

Djil took this calmly. 'If our lives and all we have depend on you explaining yourself to the Abbot, we have nothing to fear. No one can explain better than you can.'

'But who'll be the judge?' Mordec wanted to know. 'Who will say which of you has won the argument?'

'He will.'

'You'll be having to put some grand words together then,' said Delfinola.

Sam shook his head and broke the most startling part of his news. 'We must argue,' he told them, '*without saying a single word.*'

Six voices rose together 'Without *saying* anything?'

'You mean,' Djil said, 'that it must all be done in writing?'

'No. No words at all. None spoken, none written.'

'I never heard such nonsense in all m'life!' Anwid exclaimed.

'Daft he is!' wailed Delfinola.

'Fight him!' Lily said. 'Single combat.'

Gus said, 'With swords.'

'No,' said Sam. 'Swords cannot settle this matter.'

'But how in silence can you—' Djil began, shaking her head in bewilderment.

Sam shrugged. 'Gestures, symbols, actions,' he suggested. 'Each of us will try to convey what we mean, and each will try to interpret what the other tries to convey. No doubt Alonso believes he will be divinely aided to perceive the truth. I can only hope that the truth is what he does perceive.'

His listeners waited for him to say more, to tell them that it wasn't as bad as it seemed.

But the best Sam could offer was, 'Of this we can be sure. I stand as much of a chance of winning as losing.'

Mordec said, 'You'll win, Sam. You *know* more than everyone else, and you can *think* better than everyone else. You're much cleverer than *he* is.'

'Thanks, Mordec. But my fate will depend on *his* knowledge, *his* thought, *his* cleverness.' He paused for a moment as a new idea struck him. 'Strangely enough—yes, I tell you this though you'll think it strange—I'll stand a better chance of winning if I don't try to be clever at all.'

'Why d'you say that?'

'You'll see.'

'If he doesn't know when he's beaten,' Lily said, 'we'll fight to set you free, and you and Djil will come with me to England—'

'We'll hide you in the ship—' Anwid said.

'And I'll kill him,' Gus said.

'Don't be rash, good friend. The Abbot has many men—not just monks but soldiers,' Djil warned the fiery Gus.

'Get more from the mainland,' Lily said, 'and arm them. Do you have enough weapons for a few hundred fighters?'

'The Pope has legions,' Sam said. 'But it hasn't come to war. Right now we're threatened by nothing worse than an unusual sort of argument. I know I can count on your help and I may need it. But for the present, let's wait and see what happens.'

Although no boats moved between the island and the mainland, the news spread mysteriously and rapidly for miles about, that there was to be a contest between Sam and the Abbot. It was the talk of the tavern and the wayside, the hearth and the marketplace.

'Only with words,' said some.

'No, without words,' others contradicted.

'With what then?'

Nobody was sure and the uncertainty made everyone all the more curious.

Merchants and slaves sided with the Red Magician; peasants and priests with the Black Abbot. Lords and ladies were divided.

The night before the trial, Sam was fetched away to be held under guard in the church of the abbey.

'May I visit him? May our servants bring him food, make a bed for him in the church?' Djil requested.

'The abbey will supply all his needs.'

Sam was escorted by four monks and two armed guards out of his tower and in through the yawning door of the abbey. Behind them trotted Sam's three greyhounds. But the great doors of the church which shut their master in, shut the dogs out. They lay near the threshold of the church doors to wait.

'Will you let them in tomorrow when folk arrive to watch the trial?' Sam asked.

One of the monks told him that no one would be allowed to witness the trial except a few monks chosen by the Abbot. Sam was surprised to hear it.

'Did the Abbot say why?'

'Watchers cannot be trusted to be silent,' the monk replied.

'Then why do we need to be in this church? The Abbot's office would be big enough to hold him and me and a few witnesses.'

'It is here that you will be put to the test because no sorcery can be worked in a church. In this holy place even *your* black arts cannot succeed.'

'So you have pre-judged me,' Sam said. 'Why do you believe that I command black arts?'

'I've got a feeling you do,' the monk said, 'and I can tell you that when I've got a feeling about something it's hardly ever wrong. I often feel things that turn out to be absolutely right. Though I don't take any credit for it of course—it's a gift from God.'

Djil sat up all night with Anwid and Delfinola. They started a game of Eyes and Nose but found they couldn't put their minds to it.

The Duc and Duchesse of the neighboring estate of Sec-et-Doux set out in the dark and sailed to the island in their own boat which they kept in the harbour for their visits to the Gaudins. They arrived at dawn bringing a light breakfast of grapes as pale as tears and pomegranate-pips as bright as rubies. Kindly souls, they did their best to comfort Djil in her anxiety and to conceal their excitement at the unusual entertainment they were expecting.

'It is the argument between God and the Devil, my dear,' said the strong-minded Duchesse de Sec-et-Doux, 'and you know that God must win.'

'You are not saying that Sam is the Devil!' Djil exclaimed.

'No no. Only perhaps *possessed* by a devil. His soul will be set free and will fly to heaven when his body hits the rocks,' the Duchess reassured her.

The Duc, who was of a gentle disposition though a mite weak-headed, said soothingly, 'Neither of them is right, neither is wrong. These opposites must exist together. Each needs the other. Our Red Magician and our Black Abbot must live side by side in peace and harmony, as do I and my Duchesse. The balance is all. Consider the wings of butterflies. On each of a pair the pattern is turned the opposite way.'

Delfinola started to weep, and Anwid begged her please to wait for the outcome before grieving.

They all waited then as patiently as they could, until they might be allowed into the church to witness the trial.

With the same expectation of a public spectacle, townsmen, priests, piemen and alewives swarmed to the harbour and paid to be ferried across to the island, most finding standing room only in the boats. Girls from The Good Ship Good came in their own boats. Boys and pickpockets paddled themselves across the short stretch of water on whatever rafts and logs they could lay their hands on. Half a dozen of them fell into the water and those who couldn't swim were rescued by Captain Anwid's gallant girls.

The crowd hurried up the slope to the abbey gates and surged on up the steep stairs to emerge into the courtyard near the top, where the rubble of old ruins and new construction lay about and little shade was to be expected through the middle of the day. Pies and wine were on sale at once, and a jaunty fellow dressed in green invited the gentry to lay bets on their choice for a winner. '*Put* yer money on the Black Abbot,' he sang out, ''cause the power of the Church is absolute'; and a few minutes later, '*Put* yer money on Sam of the West, 'cause he's a powerful magician.'

Then on a wall which overlooked the courtyard appeared the abbey's armourer with a trumpeter beside him. The trumpeter sounded a blast and the armourer announced: 'The Abbot's orders are—listen, you rabble!—the Abbot says no one can watch the trial. Didja get that? Didja all hear me? Ya can't watch. No spectators. Ya may's well go home.'

Loud protest rose on all sides, but everyone knew better than to suppose that the Abbot could be persuaded to change his mind. The trumpeter blew another blast to silence the mob and the armourer went on: 'The trial,' he declared, 'will last three days, so don't hang about.'

'Aaaaaaah!' groaned the mob.

'Get along with yerall,' the armourer bawled, and waved his arms at them as though they were so many flies.

To the nobles and their friends, a monk took the same message. The Abbot, he told them, would hold the trial in the Abbey church with no one present but a few witnesses of his own choosing.

'But surely I can be there? I, the Duchesse de Sec-et-Doux? A devout and faithful daughter of the Church?'

'The Abbot regrets,' said the messenger, 'but his orders are *no*.'

'What have I done to be treated so cruelly?' the Duchesse wailed. Now it was her turn to be comforted and Djil's to do the comforting, while the Duc took himself off in pursuit of some sad pleasure.

Gus expected Lily to come with him to the mainland 'now that the boats are sailing again', and ride with him as they'd done on their last visit to the island. But Lily shook her head.

'I'll stay with Djil,' she said, 'until we know that Sam is safe.'

Gus strode off in anger. 'She wants to stay with Mordec,' he told himself. 'Why doesn't she just come out with it and tell me that she cares more for him than me!'

He sailed to the mainland, borrowed a strong young gelding from the Gaudins' stable and went for a long ride along the shore. But he wasn't entirely alone. An admiring gang of skiving stable-lads followed him at a respectful distance on colts and ponies, for no better reason than that Vikings were said to be savage, this one was obviously in a grumpy mood, and they hoped he'd do something perfectly frightful.

For his part, Gus seemed not to notice them, yet he never rode quite fast enough to lose them.

# the silent argument

There was nothing for Sam's grandmother, friends and greyhounds to do but wait. Mordec, wandering about the castle on his own, entered a thin tower and climbed its spiralling stairs. He noticed that some of the long openings in the thick curved wall were oddly dark, and set about discovering why. He found that a part of the adjoining abbey had been built tightly against the tower, so that these spaces, at regular intervals, were blocked in by one of its walls. Each time he rounded the stairs and came to the side where the abbey touched the tower, he put a hand through the dark hole and could feel the other wall. The last of these openings, at the top of the stairs, was wider and lighter than the rest. Beyond it he saw a small recess, like a low cave. A few buckets, a spade, a hod and some hammers had been flung into it. Cautiously he stepped into the dusty little room, and at once stepped back again on to the solid stairs of the tower. He'd seen that the wall of the cavernous space was cracked, and the long gap, though not wide enough for him to fall through, overlooked a dizzying emptiness. Telling himself that the floor was strong and he'd be in no danger, he went in again, pressed his head lightly against the split in the stone which widened towards the top, and found that he was looking down into the abbey church.

It was dim for the most part but brilliant in patches, lit by lanterns hung on chains from the curving arches, a torch or two in iron brackets on the walls, and candles flickering round the feet of statues. These lights were broken up into needles by his glasses, so at first he found it hard to see anything else, but slowly his eyes adjusted to both the dimness and the light and the scene below became clear to him. He saw Sam, standing still and alone, recognizable from above by his dark red hair. He saw the great doors open and Abbot Alonso come through them. Mordec looked down on the pink disc of scalp and the circle of yellow curls as the Abbot walked slowly with his hands pressed together against his chest. Behind him softly stepped ten monks in two lines, their hoods lying back on their shoulders so all their partly shaven heads were revealed to Mordec's view.

The doors closed again, but not before Mordec had caught sight of Sam's three greyhounds on the threshold.

Now two monks, with hoods pulled far forward over their heads, emerged from the shadows and set two chairs facing each other, a ship's width apart. The Abbot sat down and waved at Sam to do the same. The ten bare-headed monks seated themselves on benches, five in a row on each side of the Abbot. The two hooded monks set jugs of water beside the chairs. Then, making very little sound that Mordec could hear, they fetched three things and placed them between Sam and the Abbot: a tripod holding a bucket of glowing and flickering charcoal, a wooden birdcage, and something, a long bundle it seemed, wrapped in red cloth.

The Abbot rose, went to the red bundle, scooped it up and showed it to Sam. Mordec made it out to be a humanlike straw figure dressed in a cloak and hood. The Abbot strode to the fire with it, dropped it into the bucket and waited for it to catch fire. It burned brightly, sparking and crackling, until nothing was left of it but ash. Then he took a bird from the cage, held it for a moment above the fire, carried it to a high window, reached up and opened his hands. The bird flew out and up to the sky. It was a lark. Through the silence Mordec heard it singing as it soared.

The Abbot returned to his chair, and nodded to Sam. For a few moments Sam sat perfectly still. Then he leant forward—to do what? Mordec was watching so tensely that he even stopped breathing. But all Sam did was bend down, lift the water-jug from the floor, tip his head back and pour water down his throat. He put the jug down again and nodded to the Abbot.

Now the Abbot sat perfectly still. Time itself seemed to hold its breath. The candles did not flicker. The monks were motionless as statues. Sam waited, and so did Mordec in his secret nest.

At last the Abbot rose and left by a side door, followed by the monks he'd come in with. Sam remained with the two hooded monks.

Mordec retreated to the stairs and went to tell Djil, Anwid, Delfinola, Lily and Gus what he'd seen. But he held back his news until the Duc and Duchesse had gone to bed, for if the good Duchesse found out that he'd been spying, she'd be sure, he thought, to give him away to the Abbot.

So it was late when Mordec described what had happened.

Djil said: 'I don't understand what the Abbot meant, but Sam did, and his answer must have been right.'

Anwid said: 'What a lot of stuff and nonsense. Why can't this Abbot fellow come out with what's bothering him and let Sam answer him, plain and simple, loud and clear?'

Delfinola said: 'The Abbot could not have meant that a poor sinner should be cast into the fire. The Church would never do such a thing.' ('Ting', she said.)

Lily said: 'The Abbot has twelve men with him and Sam stands alone.'

Gus said: 'How big is your spy-hole, Mordec? Is it big enough for all of us to look through at the same time?'

Mordec said: 'No. And I'm not saying where it is or how I got there.'

Then Djil remembered a certain window of the castle from where it was possible to see into a window of the church. Tomorrow, she told them, she would try to catch a glimpse of what was happening in there.

Next morning Mordec was in his nest with a flask of ale and a cake in time to see the Abbot enter, followed again by ten monks. The two chairs were in place, a ship's width apart.

The Abbot sat down, then the witnesses, then Sam.

One of the guard-monks scattered something from a sack over a stretch of the stone floor, the other knelt at the abbot's feet and untied and removed his sandals. The Abbot pulled up his hood, letting it hang far forward over his face, and buried his hands in his sleeves. Barefoot, he picked his way over the stretch of floor where whatever-it-was had been strewn. He walked with small steps, big steps, sideways steps, as though performing a slow dance to music no one else could hear. At times he seemed to struggle to move at all, force himself against weakness and pain to go forward, but finally he stopped, flung back his hood, turned up a strained and weary face, so that Mordec could see his every feature, and mouthed some words. For a moment Mordec feared that those uplifted eyes must have seen him, that the Abbot was calling out, inaudibly to him, 'Spy! Spy!' But almost at once he knew that the Abbot was only praying as part of his performance.

He was right. As soon as the prayer was over, the Abbot's face was rosy-fresh again, as usual. He walked steadily to his chair and sat down. His sandals were tied on again, and he nodded solemnly. He had finished making his point.

Sam got up from his chair, went to a window and looked out. He stretched out his right arm, moved his hand from side to side, covered his eyes with it, then pressed it down on the top of his head; he dropped his arm, went back to his chair, sat down, and nodded. Again the Abbot sat still for a long time, and finally rose and departed with his ten monks.

Late that night, when the Duc and Duchesse had gone yawning to their chamber, Mordec gave Djil and the others that day's report, and Djil revealed that she had seen Sam. 'The sun was shining into a window of the church, and that's where I saw him. I believe he saw me too.'

Anwid said: 'Sheer tomfoolery on the Abbot's part if you ask me.'

Delfinola said: 'Sure I cannot tell what the Abbot or Sam may have meant, but I know that their souls were wrestling like a pair of angels.'

Lily said: 'Sam will win.'

On the third day Mordec could not see Sam or the two guard-monks anywhere in the visible part of the church, but as he was peering about for them the great double doors of bronze opened wide. The greyhounds stepped awkwardly backwards as many men came brushing past them. Two rows of monks carried someone seated on a golden throne, clothed in white and gold and wearing a three-tiered crown, such as Mordec had seen on the head of a Pope hardly older than himself who had been borne on an elephant in a great procession, to the music of drums and trumpets, through the countryside of Italy.

'The Pope has come to the island!' Mordec thought. 'He's come in person to tell the Abbot not to harm Sam.'

Yet almost at once he knew that that was not what was happening. There was something about this parade which was entirely different from the great noisy procession he had moved with from Brevis to Nebula; something that told him he was still watching the Argument rather than a true event of the Church. This was like watching jugglers and players. He thought also of Charlotte, the wonderful little dancer he had first seen at the court of the Duc and Duchesse de Sec-et-Doux, who had pretended to be a doll; and then a weird beast; and in the house of Queen Gloria had made everyone believe she was a puppet worked by strings. She had moved to music, and the music had helped the illusion. Here, now, he realized it was the *lack* of music, the quietness of a hundred men or more on the move, that gave the game away. No real Pope, he thought, would move in procession without music, but silence was the rule of the trial. As the only sounds were of soft-shod feet, rustling garments, and the creak of swinging chains, this 'Pope' was only the Abbot, and the throng that came with him—monks, boys, priests, men-at-arms—was his argument.

The boys, years younger than Mordec, were dressed in green and swung polished metal balls or tongue-less bells on chains. A musky smell reached Mordec's nose. The priests clad in gold and white and green followed the Abbot's chair. They were flanked at intervals by men in armour with feathered helmets and long cloaks fastened with gold chains.

The throne was set down so that the play-Pope faced the rest. On his lap a priest placed a book, and in each of his hands a large key. He crossed his arms on his chest. And there at last was Sam. Where had he come from? Suddenly he was standing before the Abbot, bare-foot, dressed in a dismal patched tunic that hung to his knees and reminded Mordec of a garment he had been offered for his trial in England. The idea was, he knew, to make the wearer look and feel humble and ashamed. Sam, he was glad to see, looked neither.

The Abbot gazed steadily at Sam for a long time in a silence broken only by the rustle of the fidgeting crowd. Eventually he nodded, which meant—as Mordec had learnt—that his argument was finished and it was Sam's turn to make his case without uttering a single word.

His last chance now to save his life! Mordec's heart beat faster. Calmly, Sam turned his back on the Abbot and, stretching out his arms, gestured to the crowd to part. They obeyed, some moving one way, some the other. When a clear path was open between him and the doors, Sam patted his knees and clicked his tongue. At once his three greyhounds came running to him. Panting and whimpering, they leapt up to lick his face. He pointed to the floor and down they sat, looking up at him with devoted eyes, keeping quiet and still but for a pink tongue coming out now and then to wipe a muzzle.

Sam faced the Abbot and nodded.

For a minute or two Abbot Alonso sat frowning, deep in thought. Then he shot up from his throne, hurling the keys away. They clattered loudly as they fell. The book dropped from his lap, and though a priest lunged forward to catch it he was too late and it struck the floor with a thud. The Abbot stood straight and stiff, staring at Sam as though something impossible had happened in front of his eyes. Then he strode to the great doors, brushing past Sam and the greyhounds, one of which let out a squeal as the Abbot's foot stamped, accidentally, on its tail.

A murmur broke out which swelled into a hub-bub as the monks and boys and priests and men-at-arms crowded after him, crushing one another in the doorway. When they'd all squeezed out, their noise receded. Only Sam, his two guards, and the three dogs remained. Mordec crept away.

The verdict was given next day in the abbey church. Emissaries of the Abbot had let it be known on the mainland that all and any could come and hear it, and it was a great throng that the Abbot addressed from the high pulpit.

The church was alive with excited whispering. It soon hushed when he appeared up there and frowned upon the crowd, the nobles seated in front on gild-ed chairs, the monks seated apart from the rest on benches, and Sam who stood nearest to the pulpit, alone, dressed in his own red clothes.

The Abbot's face looked so grave that Sam's friends and well-wishers stiffened with fear for him.

The hush of expectancy was broken by the Abbot's voice. 'I have heard this morning,' he said in a tone of deep solemnity, 'that our Holy Father the Pope has died.'

A murmur broke out. Djil, Anwid and Delfinola, even more anxious for Sam now, clasped each other's hands. Mordec, Gus and Lily, who were standing together in the shadow of an arch, turned questioning faces to each other. What would this mean for Sam, for themselves? Everyone's attention returned to the Abbot.

He had little more to tell about how the young Pope ('not yet eighteen years old,' he reminded them) had met his end. It had happened three days ago in Rome, where violent conflict had again been unleashed. When he, the Abbot, knew more, so would they all. They should return at four tomorrow afternoon for a requiem mass.

The Abbot half turned away. He meant to depart and let this assembly, gathered for no holy purpose, disperse. But he felt assailed by the unspoken questions of the crowd: What of Sam? Was the death of the Pope in some way due to him? Was his fate not to be known until the whole story of the Pope's death was revealed? And he asked himself: Would it be blasphemy in this solemn hour to finish the business in hand? It was not, after all, unimportant to the church. He had had time to consider if the shocking news should affect the verdict, and concluded that it should not. He turned back. The crowd shushed and held its breath.

'I shall tell you now,' he said, 'what you have come to hear.'

The crowd sighed with relief.

He started by recounting how the silent argument had run. He droned on for quite some time, and what with the heat, and the length of the exposition, many dozed off, among them Anwid and the Duc and Duchesse.

To make a long story short, this was the gist of his speech:

'On the first day I contended that when a man, signified by the puppet, has sinned, his body must perish in the purifying fire, so that his soul may fly like a lark to heaven.

'The accused replied that the grace of God may be poured like pure water into every man and cleanse even the worst of sinners.

'I went away and thought about his answer and knew that he was right. But still he had to justify his ways, his probing into secrets that God has chosen not to make plain to mankind.

'So on the second day I contended that the path we must tread through life is thorny, that this world is a vale of pain and tears, through which we must struggle with God's help.

'He replied—by going to the sunny window and putting a hand over his eyes and then on his head—that we do not strive in darkness. The light by which we see is from God, and our understanding is from God, and by His grace we thrive under the sun.

'I went away and thought about his answer and knew that he was right. But still he had to prove that he, Sam of the West, known throughout the civilized world as the Red Magician, had the right to express opinions which challenge the authority of the Church.

'So on the third day I contended that he was a humble, powerless creature and the one true authority in this world is the Church, and the duty of every mortal creature is to obey it; and only that is right and true which the Church decrees is right and true.

'Then he, by summoning the dogs, replied that God gave man authority over the beasts and all the other creatures of the earth, to name, to tend and to use until the end of time.

'I was angry at first because I thought he was trying to slide out of the charges against him by making a slick point the way cunning lawyers do. But I pondered his answer for many hours, and prayed for guidance. Again, finally, I knew that *he was right.*'

Mordec thought that the Abbot's case, as he'd explained it, had been neither *interesting* nor *reasonable*. But what he said next was fine.

'Therefore, Sam Gaudin, you are acquitted of all wrongdoing. Your life is spared, and you may carry on with the work you have been doing, which I declare to be not sinful, and you may hold your lands and possessions in peace and safety.'

Some of the crowd broke into applause, but despite the racket Mordec heard a door near him open and close. He went to it, looked out, and saw Forl scurrying off down a long dimly torchlit hall. The flaming torches threw a multitude of his shadows on the floor and walls, flitting like wraiths in panic back to an underworld home. Mordec was not at all surprised at the man's sudden wish to flee.

He stepped back into the church to watch the Abbot and monks and boys depart in procession. He saw the Abbot speaking into the ear of his closest attendant, and guessed what he might be saying.

Mordec's guess was almost precisely right.

'Find Forl,' the Abbot was whispering. 'Bring him to me. This time he will tell me the truth.'

Mordec waited, as Sam did, for the crowd to leave. When he thought they were alone at last, he came out of his comer and was about to speak; but two monks emerged from another of the arches and made their way slowly towards Sam, so he waited.

One of the two was Brother Nico, the other was guiding him. The blind monk raised his bony hands to feel Sam's face, hair, shoulders, arms, and hands.

'I am glad—to have met you—Sam Gaudin. You are one who—will illumine—our age for generations—yet unborn. It has been—an ordeal—for you, this trial. But—God has given you—your gifts. May you—use them always—for the good of your fellow—men.'

He was led away. Mordec and Sam and the greyhounds left the church together. At last Mordec was able to tell Sam how he'd witnessed the proceedings and kept the others informed of what he saw, and how baffled they had all been by the silent argument.

In their large round room Djil embraced Sam, exclaiming, 'What a relief!' Lily embraced him too, and Gus shook his hand. Anwid complimented him on his 'performance', and Delfinola wept. She said her tears were 'at the same time both of sorrow for the Holy Father and of joy for Sam'.

Mordec asked Sam what they were all burning to know: how he'd understood the Abbot's arguments and how he'd known the right answers; and how he'd worked out the actions to convey his points so tellingly to the Abbot. Sam promised to explain when they were round the dining table.

The Duc and Duchesse had set off home as soon as the verdict was out.

Djil apologised for the 'plain fare' on the table. 'I could not have it festive,' she said, 'because the day has its sorrow too.'

'Of course,' Mordec said, keeping his face as serious as Djil's did hers, while his eyes roved happily over the meats and the birds, the fishes, the fruits, the cakes and the choicest of wines.

They sat down to it, and Sam told them his side of the story.

'On the first day I watched Alonso do whatever he wanted to. I sat still until he'd finished. By the time he'd been through his rigmarole I was hot and thirsty, so I had a drink.

'On the second day his carry-on was even longer and more tedious. When he'd done I got up to stretch my legs, looked out of the window and saw you, Grandmother, at a window of the castle. So I waved, and put my hand over my eyes and on my head to suggest that if you came out it would be a good idea to put on a shady hat.

'On the third day when the parade came through the doors I couldn't see if the dogs were still there. When my time came to act I got everyone to move aside so I could look for them. And there they were.' He stroked their ears fondly. 'I patted my knee and they came to me. That's all.'

First Mordec laughed, then Lily, then Djil, then all except Gus who was even more puzzled by Sam's explanation than he had been by the Abbot's.

'So you didn't *know*,' he said, 'what it *meant* when you drank, and waved, and covered your eyes, and touched your head, and got the dogs in?'

'I knew what *I* meant,' Sam said. 'I meant to quench my thirst, I meant to tell Grandmother to put on a hat, and I meant to bring the dogs in. But what really mattered was not what I meant but *what the Abbot would think I meant*. He's the one who goes in for elaborate argument in signs and actions, not I. Before we began I guessed that I could do anything at all and simply leave the interpretation to him, and I'd stand as much of a chance of getting off as of being condemned. Even slightly more of a chance. Because, you see, all the argument would go on in his own head, and the less that came from me to disturb his thoughts, the better.'

'So that's why you told us it would be better not to try and be too clever!' Mordec said.

'But he might equally well have decided that his argument was better than yours,' Anwid objected.

'Not quite,' Sam said. 'He'd be afraid of people thinking that he hadn't understood me. Then they might think he wasn't as clever as I am. So you see, it isn't that I've proved myself innocent, it's that he's proved himself—'

'Brilliant,' Anwid said.

'And just,' Mordec said, and they all laughed except Gus, who looked from one to another, bewildered again.

'And just,' Sam repeated seriously. 'Let's give him the benefit of any doubt and say that he really did mean to be just.'

Gus shook his head, unconvinced and even more confused. But Mordec, Lily, Djil, and Anwid nodded, and Delfinola said, so sweetly that it was almost as if she were singing, 'You are a lovely man, Sam Gaudin.'

'Did the death of the Pope affect the verdict, do you think?' his grandmother asked.

'It's still very bare news,' Sam said. 'I would have received it before the Abbot if I had not been shut away. I know that he was assassinated. I think it will take not weeks or months but years for that web of intrigue to be unravelled, if ever it can be. And we shouldn't imagine we've escaped it. It isn't over. The Pope's death might make our Abbot stronger and more ambitious.'

# thor's hammer

Before he went to bed, Sam took Anwid and Delfinola up to his watch-room, spread charts before them, and told them what they might expect on the voyage across the channel to England.

'A treacherous season,' he warned them. 'The reports are of tempests, sudden, strong, soon over, but if you are blown off course in this direction, you may be caught by an unusual surface drift and be carried as far as *here*, where a narrower but even stronger current at a slight depth could bear you this way, how far I cannot say—'

Anwid looked and listened and made sketches of her own. As she rolled up her parchments she said, 'You are a boon to mariners, Sam Gaudin. I thank you. Now we'd better get some sleep.'

'There'll be the tide to catch at the shiver of dawn,' Delfinola said, suppressing a yawn.

Sam lighted them to their chamber doors, then went to Mordec's and knocked.

'You'll be sailing early,' he said when Mordec looked out. 'Come now and show me this nest of yours.'

'Will you close the holes in the wall?' Mordec asked as they set off, each with a tall candle.

'Perhaps—and perhaps not,' Sam replied, casting a brief but meaningful glance at Mordec, who nodded.

Mordec led the way. Their candles, flickering in the draught, threw fantastic shadows on the walls, looming and darting, stretching and shrinking, cavorting and trembling. Mordec and Sam moved quietly, but the greyhounds followed on clicking paws.

Gus heard the clicking pass his door. 'Only the dogs,' he told himself, and was about to get into bed when he saw a piece of parchment on his pillow. He held it near the candle and frowned. It was some kind of map with a twisting row of arrows, drawn in smudgy charcoal. There was no writing on it. Had there been words he could have taken it to Mordec to find out what they were. Perhaps this map-maker could not write. Or knew that he—Gus—could not read. He wondered if it could be from Lily. Did she want him to meet her somewhere?

Because he would have liked it to be from Lily, he decided it was. So he set about trying to understand the drawing and the arrows, staring at it for some time. At last his frown cleared away. He bound his shoes on, took his candle and left his chamber, closing the oaken door quietly behind him.

Through other doors he heard snoring or the unintelligible words of a sleep-talker in a troubled dream. He pressed his ear to Lily's but heard not a sound. He went to Mordec's and did the same, and again heard nothing.

Following what he had made out to be the route of the arrows, he descended to the gates. The guards knew him.

'Did the English queen come out of the tower?' he asked them.

'No,' a guard replied.

How, Gus wondered, had Lily got to the abbey church without them seeing her? For that was clearly where the arrows pointed to.

'I'll be back soon,' he said. 'Probably with the queen. What's the password tonight?'

'Trust not,' one of the guards whispered in his ear.

Gus nodded. 'A good tip,' he said.

There were no guards at the abbey gates, which stood wide open, as did the main doors. Wall-torches lit the cavernous space beyond.

The bronze doors of the church were closed, but when he pushed hard against them they yielded without a creak, and he passed through into a space so large that the torches and candles could light only parts of it, banking up the night in the recesses under the arches. Gus set his own candle down where others burned before a stone statue. He was frowning again in perplexity, not because the church was lit though empty—he knew the monks came every few hours to chant and pray—but because he could not imagine what had brought Lily here. She could have chosen a nearer, pleasanter place for them to meet. Probably the choice was not hers. Others were involved and she must need his help.

'Lily?' he said, not too loudly, advancing, stopping, listening, advancing again. 'Lily, where are you?'

He heard a rustle, a footfall behind him and whirled round with a greeting ready on his lips, but gasped instead as a masked and bulky figure bore down on him with both arms raised, holding aloft an axe, its blade catching the orange-red light and flashing as it descended towards his head to split it in two.

He dodged and leapt backwards, and the blade went down to hit the floor with a clang of metal on stone. The assailant, groaning with fury, lifted it again, and in another moment would have succeeded in murdering Gus most brutally and bloodily, had not something crashed onto his own skull and felled him instantly.

Gus stared at the cloaked body lying so still. Frozen, he stood and watched a pool of blood spreading over the floor. Not another sound came from the fallen man. It was unlikely that of his own will he would ever stir again. He was dead. Slain. And near him lay the instrument of his death, a large and heavy hammer. It had been hurled down from above by an invisible hand. It could only have been the hand of Thor.

Gus, overcome with awe, looked up to the high roof of the church as if he might see the god hovering there. 'Thor!' he whispered. 'Thank you for saving my life!'

Only then, his heart still beating wildly, he turned the body over and pulled off the mask.

'Forl.' The deceptively benign face of the treacherous servant was unmistakable.

Now Gus understood. Of course, Forl had wanted revenge. Dangerous as it was for him to stay on the island when the Abbot's men were looking for him, he'd risked it for the chance of getting back at Gus, who more than any one else, he might think, was to blame for spoiling his mission and putting him in jeopardy.

He had drawn the map. He had put it on Gus's pillow. He had been in his chamber this night, Gus thought with a shudder.

'Forl could have hidden there in the daytime and attacked me while I was sleeping. Why didn't he do that? It would have been easier and safer for him.'

Then Gus remembered the greyhounds. No interloper could hide in Sam's castle after dark while they were on watch. So he had lured his quarry here, and now this would-be murderer lay dead.

No doubt the Abbot would be angry that he could not question Forl, make him confess who had masterminded the plot and written the false letter. But Gus was unconcerned about that. He was too full of relief and gratitude to care about other matters. The gods watched over him and preserved him! He was destined by them for some great task, just as he'd always supposed he was. This thought held him here, in the place of fear and wonder, for minutes on end when he should have fled as fast as he could.

'No one can connect me with the dead body,' he reasoned with is fear. 'Anyway, I didn't kill him.

Perhaps when they see the hammer they'll understand that our gods are mightier than theirs.'

Then at last he started in haste for the open doorway, but stopped as two figures appeared in it. He caught his breath—the monks! They would find him here with the corpse.

But he breathed again. The two people illuminated waveringly by candles and torches were Mordec and Sam. The dogs followed them in.

Gus went to meet them.

'Something happened here tonight,' he began in a low, urgent tone, meaning to prevent them from taking another step until he had warned them what to expect and given them a few words of explanation.

But Sam walked straight to where Forl lay, as if he'd come here for that very purpose. He looked first at the body, then at the axe, and then at the hammer.

'It's Forl, and that's what killed him,' Gus said. 'Thor's hammer. It dropped from above. Forl was trying to kill me with the axe when Thor killed him.'

'I see,' Sam said. 'Come away now, Gus. I'll talk to the Abbot about this after you've sailed. Which must be soon.'

And before Gus could say another word he pulled him by the sleeve and led him and Mordec out to the steep path and on to where his own guards waited with lanterns.

They went to Mordec's chamber, and when the door was closed, Gus tried again to tell his story, but

111

Sam stopped him with a statement so astonishing that he fell quiet and listened to all that Sam had to tell him about the happening in the abbey church. Gus stared at him in disbelief.

'You mean to say that *you* dropped the hammer on Forl?'

'No, *Mordec* did,' Sam corrected him firmly. 'We saw him coming for you, and Mordec dropped the hammer on him.'

'It was hard to aim,' Mordec said. 'The slit in the wall up there is narrow, and I couldn't lean out far, and he was moving. I'd like to think it was because I aimed well, but I suppose it was just luck that I hit him square on the head.

'It wasn't luck, it was Thor. Thor guided the hammer to save me. I know he did.'

'If you like,' Mordec said, laughing.

As usual, Gus couldn't see anything funny in what had happened or in what Mordec had said.

'It was a *hammer*,' he said, turning to Sam. 'Thor's own weapon,' he explained to the so-called Red Magician who was supposed to know everything yet apparently had no knowledge or understanding of the Norse gods.

He turned back to Mordec. 'But—all right, you dropped it. You meant to save my life and you did, even if you couldn't have done it without Thor. So we're even, Mordec, you and I. I helped save your life in England, and now you've helped save mine.'

Mordec, puzzled as to why Gus was scowling when he should be feeling relieved, raised both hands as though to ward off gushes of gratitude, and said in a tone of mock protest, 'Enough, enough of your thanks.'

'I just want you to remember—that's all,' Gus said, 'We're quits. Even. Remember that, Mordec.'

'I'll remember. Right. You don't owe me anything.'

'I don't owe you anything? I'm not so sure about that,' Gus said, but neither Mordec nor Sam could guess his meaning.

On Sam's advice, The Good Ship Good sailed before 'the shiver of dawn', and it was well for Mordec and Gus that she did. For even as they were leaving the harbour, the monks were entering their church two by two, chanting, and came upon the corpse lying in its blood before the altar, and two by two they stopped their chanting until there was an awful silence.

'What has happened?' Brother Nico hoarsely asked his neighbour.

When the Abbot had made sure who it was who lay there in his own blood, and that he was dead, he went himself to the blind man and broke the news to him.

Gently he led him to the body. Brother Nico knelt beside it, spread his fingers on the cold face of his servant, and wept. 'Forl! My poor Forl!—Who could have—done this—to you?'

'Who indeed?' the Abbot asked, expecting no answer. He tried to comfort Brother Nico. 'We shall find out the truth,' he promised.

He dispatched two monks to question the guards at Sam's gate. A young monk picked up the axe, saw its clean blade and laid it down; hefted the hammer, exclaimed at its weight, and asked his god for mercy on the soul of the dead man. (Gus would have been disappointed to know that it did not suggest the name of Thor to him or anyone else.)

Brother Nico said, speaking with even more strain than usual, 'I do not—believe that my good Forl—ever meant—to do anything bad. He—was always good—to me—beyond the call—of duty. A hidden hand is at work. He was—afraid perhaps—that harm would be done—to me if he did not—obey the evil instructions. Or perhaps he was—persuaded—that—substituting the forged letter—would bring—some good to me. And now will we—ever know? The hidden hand—has a long reach—and has silenced him forever.'

The Abbot's messengers returned, bringing the only information the guards were willing to impart: that the English ship had sailed.

'Then the Vikings—have gone,' Brother Nico said, almost inaudibly.

But the Abbot heard and answered him: 'My dear Brother, do not despair. Remember that the Church has a very long arm and can reach everywhere on land and sea.'

# perils of the sea

The Good Ship Good had slipped her moorings in a brisk pre-dawn breeze, which kept up well into the day. For some hours the sun warmed her timbers and the sailor-girls washed her decks with brine and giggled over nothing in particular.

Lily took a turn at the rudder under instruction from the Mate and encouragement from Gus.

Mordec, in the low space under the foredeck, re-packed his books ready for disembarking. The six pairs of glasses his grandfather had given him, each in its own wooden box, he placed side by side on top of everything else, moving quietly because the girls who'd been on the night-watch in the harbour were sleeping in a row of bundles, leaving the doors open for fresh air.

Then he went to drop his fishing lines. 'If I fill a bucket with fish,' he thought, 'we could smoke them when we land. Food for the journey north. We'll be more than a day on the road to the East Fenreach.'

He took off his cloak and his scrip and left them with his books in the hatch.

But before he had baited his first hook, a black cloud hooded the sun. More clouds were looming, heavy with rain.

The sea darkened to purple, the breeze suddenly dropped. A hush fell over the water, so ominous that even the laughing sailor-girls fell silent. When the wind blew again it was angry, rising quickly to a gusty roar. The sails flapped and tugged at their restraining ropes. Delfinola seized the rudder, ignoring Lily's shout that she could hold it. The Captain climbed to the poopdeck calling out orders in her strong voice, the Mate repeated them sharply, and the girls scurried about, stumbling and staggering each time the ship heaved on the mounting billows.

'*All* hands to the masts,' the Captain cried. Delfinola went to rouse the sleeping girls. They came crawling out of their shelter just as the rain began to fall. At once they went to work. So did Mordec and Gus and Lily, lying on the cross-beams to help furl the sails. They slid to the deck in haste as the ship began to tilt drastically. In a few moments they were sodden.

Mordec and Gus sat holding on to the mainmast, and Lily tied herself to it with her belt. Peering through his wet glasses, Mordec thought he saw Black Monks on the deck, but soon made out that these were members of the crew who had put on hooded capes soaked in black fish-oil. Awkward in their heavy wraps, the girls tottered about and were hurled down as the wind took a hard hold of the ship and dragged her off her course.

Now the Mate found the rudder useless even in her strong hands, and the Captain, for all her prompt and correct action, and all her experience in these waters, could do nothing to wrest her craft from the clutches of the storm. It tipped the broad ship sideways until her masts stretched out over the water like fishing rods, and hung there between loss and recovery.

Mordec thought, 'Which will it be—masts down into the sea and all of us drowning, or up into the air and all of us saved?' Up they swung into the frantic, screaming air, to rock and topple again. And all the while the ship was being dragged through an early darkness towards treacherous coasts, hidden shoals, or unknown waters.

A glowing rift appeared in the thick sky, not as a glimmer of hope but a warning that it was evening and night was on its way.

When all was black, and the storm still pulling and tossing the ship, knocking her about as if she weighed no more than a fishing-boat, the Captain struggled to the side and clung there harkening for another dread sound beneath the tumult of wind and sea, the sound of doom itself, timber tearing on rock.

For an age or so it seemed to her, she stood waiting for the worst. Then almost as suddenly as it had arisen, the storm stopped. The wind's howl dropped to a moan and died away. The waves calmed, the ship was almost still, and the sailor-girls, shedding their black cloaks, rose and looked up at the sky. Mordec looked up too and saw stars breaking out. The masts swayed gently across them.

Captain Anwid's voice was hoarse as she ordered some of the girls back to their rest and others to spread the sails, which soon hung white in the star-light though no wind came to fill them. The last of the cloud thinned, took on rainbow colours, and parted to reveal a yellow moon which spread its light like butter on the wet deck.

'If I knew where we were,' the Captain said to the Mate, 'we could start rowing. But danger could be lying all round us. We must wait for the morning.'

The Mate, the boys and Lily rolled themselves in oiled capes and went to sleep. Girls stood drooping at their posts, still dazed by the fury of the storm. Mordec went back to baiting a hook for fishing in the dark.

'Lanterns,' the Captain ordered. 'Hop to it! Five to each mast, thirty on the decks bows to stern. Inspect ship and cargo for damage.'

There were other seafarers in those waters who did know where they were, men who knew those seas as well as they knew their own limbs; captains who could find their way through the blackest night, and could never be blown to any patch that was not part of their own foam-farm and brine-meadow.

Such a one came nosing through the eerie stillness of the night, turning his longship's prow this way and that like an hyena sniffing for the trail of its prey. No lantern swung on his mast. No sailor of his dared sneeze or clear his throat. Stealthily he came, his oarsmen pulling with slow powerful strokes, near and nearer to The Good Ship Good, every oar muffled and weighted on its dipping end with the carcass of a cormorant. Behind him he trailed a smaller vessel, empty. Those who had been sailing in it had moved to the bigger ship where they waited, still and silent, for his orders.

He hove to on the leeside of The Good Ship Good where no moonpath wavered on the water. And he smiled, for she was his chosen quarry. He knew this big tub of a ship by her size and shape. Unmistakably this was she, lit up now with a constellation of small lights as if to welcome him.

Captain Anwid herself was the first to see the intruders. Strolling to where they had drawn in silently alongside, she caught sight of the smaller ship. Its very emptiness alerted her. The instinct of a seasoned sailor made her look over the side to see the other ship which must be there laden with pirates. At that very moment the pirate-captain looked up, and for a second he and she stared into each other's eyes.

'To arms!' she cried, straightening up, and making a trumpet of her hands. 'Battle stations, blow the whistle, strike the gong, rouse the sleepers, break out weapons, take your stands! Bring me my bow and my sword!'

Now the daily drilling of the crew proved its worth as the girls responded instantly, without panic although unsure whether this was a test or their first real crisis. Clamor rose on all sides, from throats and whistle and gong.

Weapons were in the hands of the defenders before the pirate-captain had finished cursing and spitting in his fury at being spotted too soon. But his signal for attack wasn't long delayed. A screeching gull-cry rose from his throat and his pirates sprang into fierce action. In a trice their grappling-hooks were flying upwards. With a banging and clanging, iron gripped wood, and the pirates, shrieking, yelling, barking, or howling like whipped dogs swarmed up the ropes to the deck of The Good Ship Good. Some of them wore helmets, some were bareheaded, all of them were hung about with arsenals of knives, short-swords, chains, spikes and hammers.

Above them stood Anwid and her archers taking aim and shooting straight and hard onto the helmet-ed heads of the first raiders. Seven arrows swished downward, and seven pirates fell back into their own ship. But others reached the deck beyond the arch-ers, where the rest of the crew waited in line with drawn swords. Their eyes were fixed on Delfinola's hand, raised ready to signal a counter-attack. Behind them Lily waited, holding her sword low, willing though not eager to fight; while Gus on her right and Mordec on her left had the light of battle in their eyes. They stood firmly balanced, their swords upright before their faces. They watched pirates leap-ing on the archers and knocking them down. The Captain had flung her bow away and was swinging her sword with wide strong sweeps, keeping four enemies at bay.

Down came Delfinola's hand, and the girls, ut-tering their practiced cries of hate and fury, slashed, cut and thrust with an energy that matched their attackers'. Almost at once they became aware that these enemies were not men but boys, of much the same age as themselves, though bigger. The sound they heard now was a chorus of cheers, jeers and laughter from a new wave of huge yellow-haired men who had climbed on board but were standing back, bristling with weapons, urging the boys on.

The laughing, painted faces were caught by the lanternlight and Gus saw one clearly, then another, and another. He gasped and lowered his sword. But Mordec brought his clashing against another in the hand of one of the boys. As the two weapons locked and the fighters, in one stride, came so close together that they almost knocked nose with nose, their eyes widened, they stared at each other and froze. Both lowered their swords.

'Mordec?' the attacker said, stepping back.

'Olaf?' said Mordec. 'Odds-bods! It's you.'

'And odds-bods it's you!' Olaf said. 'But what are you—' They broke into astonished laughter, stopped, started again, and began slapping each other on the shoulder as if they had never been anything but the best of friends. A moment more and they were surrounded by boys, among them Eric, Gunnar and Big Hengist, all laughing at the surprise of this meeting.

'Yeee-ow!' Gus howled, then Eric and Gunnar with him, 'Yeeeeee-ow!' The three of them spread their arms, clasped one another's shoulders and stamped a dance of triumph and abandon. Big Hengist, Olaf and Mordec would have joined in, but the pirate-captain shouted at them to 'disarm the enemy!', and all except Mordec and Gus rushed into the fray.

It didn't take the Vikings long to overwhelm the girls and wrest their weapons from them.

The watching men had stopped laughing when they saw the boys pause in their fighting to howl and dance. Lumbering forward, curious but cautious, they'd tried to find out was happening. Before they knew anything, combat had started again.

But it did not last long. Only three or four defenders fought on after the girls were disarmed, among them Anwid, who had not wavered for an instant. Keeping her eyes narrowed and her chin up, she thrust and sliced tirelessly. When the pirate-captain held his sword out to one side, raised his free hand in the sign of truce, and shouted 'Enough!', her opponent leapt back beyond her reach, and only then did she notice that the battle was over and she and her girls had lost. Making a quick choice between death and surrender, she bent, placed her sword on the deck, and stood up again, meeting the pirate-captain's triumphant smile with an expression of emotionless dignity. Those few of her girls who still held weapons followed her example in giving them up, but preferred to drop them noisily, in protest, rather than lay them down quietly. They clattered onto the deck, and boys swaggered over to pick them up.

Only Delfinola, though her blade had been knocked from her hand early on, would still not admit defeat. She went on hitting a thickly-bearded wild-haired fellow on the top of his head with a ladle. He parried her blows with an open hand, smiling all the while. 'Take that, and that, and that,' she roared.

'Enough, Delfinola,' the Captain called to her. 'It's over. Let him go.'

'Oh no lady!' the hairy man cried to Delfinola. 'Don't stop, keep on, let's dance!' He wobbled and stamped, to roar after roar of laughter from the massed pirates.

But Delfinola reluctantly obeyed her Captain, and with a look of unconquerable contempt she hurled her ladle at the man's bristling face. Laughing, he raised his arms, ducked, and let it glance off his elbow.

Olaf looked round for Gus and Mordec, and found Gus at his side.

'So, Olaf,' Gus said, 'it was true what you said about Bjarwulf letting you sail with him!'

Olaf said, pointing to the pirate-captain, 'There he is—Bjarwulf son of Bjarwulf.'

Gus gazed at the famous man with awe. He had seen him before, but only at a distance. He remembered him as being bigger. But he was impressive enough. His head was bald but for a clump of hair sprouting from its crown like a horse's tail, tied with a thong and pierced with a jewelled arrow. Two thin strands hung like icicles from his upper lip to his knees. He wore only short breeches, stiff and stained by the sea, and heavy boots, and two leather belts holding swords and knives and iron spikes. His otherwise bare body shone with oil and ornaments: gold loops in his ears and nose, necklaces, armbands and finger-rings, all studded with enormous precious stones. On his muscular back were painted creatures of the deep in many colours.

Now he, Bjarwulf, one of the greatest of the noble Vikings who ever won glory on the sea by massacre and plunder, stuck his thumbs in his belt and sauntered over to talk to Gus. Gus drew in a deep breath and stood as tall as he could.

'Vikings on an English ship?' Bjarwulf said. 'Captives?'

'No, Bjarwulf son of Bjarwulf, we are passengers.'

'So you know who I am,' Bjarwulf said. 'Tell me who you are.'

'I am Gus son of Hakon.'

'And this is Mordec son of Hauk,' Olaf proclaimed, his hand on Mordec's shoulder as though to show off a prized possession.

'Vikings on a tub like this!' Bjarwulf said. He leant back and guffawed, and all his men and boys guffawed with him. So did Mordec, because he enjoyed their laughter, but not Gus, who wanted urgently to explain why they were here.

'We're sailing to England—' he began.

Bjarwulf cut him short.

'Tell me later, lad.'

Raising his voice he ordered the men and boys to 'strip this ship and take the girls for slaves.'

He looked at Gus again. 'And you, Gus son of Hakon, can kill the Captain and the other old woman.'

'No!'

It was Mordec who dared to shout this at the great man. He ran and stood in front of Anwid.

'No, Bjarwulf son of Bjarwulf! *They* were ready to die for us, now *we* must—'

'Ah well,' Bjarwulf said regretfully, 'leave it then. We'll take the lot of them alive. And who's this?'

Gus spoke up. 'She's Lily—'

'I'll speak for myself,' Lily said. Raising her voice and looking Bjarwulf in the eyes, she declared, 'I am Lily, Queen of the East Fenreach, and your sworn enemy. But I have no quarrel with you now if you will promise to put me down safely on the shore of England.'

'You make demands as though you had power to force me.'

'She's under *my* protection,' Gus announced.

'Mine,' said Mordec. 'She asked *me* to go with her to find her mother who'd been captured by Ingolf son of Eyiolf.'

He was looking at Bjarwulf and didn't see the fury that came into Gus's face.

'You'll put us all on an English shore if you please, Captain Bjarwulf,' said Anwid. 'We're no use to you, you know, my Mate and I—'

'And the girls? What d'you want me to do with them, since I'm granting everyone's wishes?'

'They stay with us.'

But Bjarwulf had lost interest in the women and girls for the present.

'Whatever's on this ship—take it if its worth taking!' he ordered.

The pirates, young and old, ran caterwauling to seize everything they could lay their hands on.

Gus and Mordec stood watching them uneasily.

'Come on you two, give us a hand,' Olaf called to them.

But still they stood and watched.

When Bjarwulf heard what cargoes the ship was carrying, he clutched his ears and screamed in a thin, high-pitched voice, 'Straw? Garlic? Samphire? Green wine?'

'That's it,' Anwid said. 'So you see, you don't get much for your trouble. You've made a silly mistake, you know. My ship never carries anything worth the risk of a fight. Haven't you heard of The Good Ship Good? *Everyone* knows we are not worth attacking.'

'Forget the straw,' Bjarwulf yelled full-voiced again. 'Take the samphire and the wine!' Then he asked himself, 'And the garlic? I don't know. Lars!' he bawled at a lanky pirate whose whole head was covered by a helmet made of iron strips like a birdcage. 'Lars, get Pelf up here.'

A few moments later a small, thin-haired, skinny-limbed man, dressed in a clean tunic and polished shoes, was helped from the pirate ship onto the deck of The Good Ship Good. He stood peering about with an expression of distaste.

'We're taking the samphire and green wine,' Bjarwulf told him.

'That's *all*? Nothing else?' the peppery little man said, lifting his shoulders, spreading his arms and turning up the palms of his hands.

'Well, there's straw,' Bjarwulf said, hesitantly. 'I told them, leave the straw.'

'Where, show me! That's the straw? In wooden crates? And cooped with *tin*? *Straw* under *tin*? You,' he said, looking at Delfinola, 'are either a very rich or a very stupid woman. The cover's worth more than the stuff it's covering, you bonehead.'

'*I*'m the Captain,' Anwid said. 'And I don't have to explain myself to you.'

The ferocious little man turned back to Bjarwulf and shook a finger up at him. 'Take the tin *and* the straw.'

'You're sure, Pelf? The straw's bulky and not worth—'

'Didn't you hear me—?' Pelf scolded. 'I said take it. You want my advice or not?'

'Yes, of course. Take the straw!' Bjarwulf shouted. 'And the garlic. Pelf? What about the garlic?'

'Garlic? Of course. Garlic will pay if you can get it to London or Hedeby.'

'Won't the longship be too crowded?' Lars asked Bjarwulf. 'Why don't we just take the ship with everything and everyone on it?'

Pelf heard. 'You want the ship? Bjarwulf!' He stamped his feet. 'I'm asking you—do you want the ship or not?'

'Hmm,' Bjarwulf said. He looked up at the masts, scratched his bald head as he gazed at the raised decks fore and aft, and examined the rudder. He jiggled it, tried to lift it, and finding he couldn't, kicked it. Pelf waited with tightened lips and impatient eyes, tapping one foot.

'No,' Bjarwulf told him. 'The ship's too heavy, too deep, too slow to turn. And the rudder's fixed in the stern. No. It's only good for women and girls to play with.'

'An Englishman might buy it,' Pelf said, not sounding too sure.

'I'll ransom it myself if you put me ashore and give me three days,' Anwid said quickly.

'You?' Bjarwulf shook his head. 'You have gold ready?'

'No, but I can get it if you give me time.'

'No time. Time seems always to mean never. No, I'll put you two women and the queen on an empty shore and push off.'

'Sell it somewhere else then?' Lars suggested.

'Where? It could take years to find someone stupid enough to buy this tub.'

'But the timber! It's all good stuff!' Pelf fumed.

'Where'll we break it up?'

'The sensible thing for you to do,' Anwid said, 'is take the cargo and leave us to sail the ship home.'

'You and who?'

'My Mate and the gels.'

'No, no!' Pelf whined, hunching his back. 'Not the girls. We must sell the girls or keep them. Good strong slaves, Bjarwulf! When we're talking girls we're talking money.'

Bjarwulf turned back to Anwid. 'We keep the girls and burn the ship. To tell you the truth, this wasn't really meant to be a real plunder attack. It was only to train the boys. But Pelf won't let me leave cargo behind.'

'Train the boys?'

'Pirates have to be taught like everybody else,' Bjarwulf said. 'Prentices need practice whatever trade they're learning. These boys are just starting out in life and this is their very first raid. That's why we chose your ship.'

'You *chose* my ship? So you knew it, you knew who we were and what sort of thing we carried?'

'More or less. I knew you'd be an easy capture for my boys' first go.'

'I never thought of that,' Anwid confessed to Delfinola sorrowfully. The two women comforted each other with the good news that none of their crew had been killed or badly hurt. Delfinola doctored the wounded girls, and a very old Viking with shaking hands bandaged the heads and limbs of boys, while unhurt girls looked on, finding some satisfaction in watching the victors bleed.

When the question of what to take was settled more or less to Pelf's satisfaction, taken it was, and there was nothing more to delay them.

The men saw Anwid, Delfinola, and Lily into their longship. The boys herded some of the girls over the longship and crammed them into Foal of the Foam. Olaf shouted for Gus and Mordec to come with him, but he got no answer and he couldn't see either of them.

'Courage, gels!' Anwid called down to the maidens huddled together in the smaller ship, and they waved and smiled.

Lars, ordered to burn The Good Ship Good, got the idea that the quickest and easiest way to set her alight was simply to throw down all the lanterns and let them spill their flaming oil. Spilt straw caught first, and soon there were fires burning merrily all over the decks.

Mordec was in the space under the foredeck looking for his baggage and precious books until it occurred to him that it must all have been taken as loot. He wasn't troubled. 'I'll find it and they'll let me have it,' he told himself as he backed, bent over, towards the doors—which he had not yet reached when he was hit hard on the head. He fell and lay still. The hand that had struck the stunning blow pulled his glasses off.

Shrouded in a hooded raincloak, the assailant closed the doors and took some minutes to block them with a heavy water-barrel.

Minutes later, Lars took a last looked round The Good Ship Good, and being sure that there was nobody left on board but himself, shouted 'Watch out below!', released the last grappling hook, and jumped into the longship.

'What is the name of this ship?' Delfinola asked Pelf.

Pelf looked her up and down as though to put a price on her.

'Serpent King,' he said. 'And what's yours?'

'My name? When you've found it out you can talk to me. Until then—pfui!'

'Pull away!' Bjarwulf ordered.

Lily squeezed her way about the longship asking if anyone had seen Mordec, 'the one with the glasses'.

'Glasses?' an oarsman said. 'I saw him go to the other ship with the boys.'

'Is Mordec there?' she called to Olaf who was standing in the prow of the small ship.

By the light of the moon Olaf surveyed the boys and girls crammed into Foal of the Foam and saw a figure under a rain-cloak, his face half-hidden, but with glasses which distinctly caught the light. Lily saw the glint of them too.

'Yes—he's here,' Olaf shouted. 'You coming over?'

She considered. 'No,' she called back.

She would stay on Serpent King with Anwid and Delfinola.

The pirates pushed their oars against the broad hull of The Good Ship Good whose decks were now burning with many fires; and the boys in Foal of the Foam pushed theirs against the side of Serpent King, to which, however, they remained attached by a rope.

Lily found Captain Anwid standing straight, her gaze fixed on The Good Ship Good, not with sorrow but with pride. Lily knew better than to say anything. After a while she lay down to sleep, but the Captain watched on through the night, until her fiery ship faded in the dawn and dissolved in the morning.

# eyes and nose

As a steady breeze wafted her home, Lily stood on Serpent King waiting for the first glimpse of the English coast, and thinking that if Bjarwulf should be on the battlefield in her war against the Vikings, she would have him brought to her alive, and she would either herself devise an end for him which would be a warning to all pirates, or she would hand him over to Anwid to have that pleasure, provided that her father sent soldiers to the war. How, she wondered, would Anwid choose to execute him?

'Lily!'

Gus was hailing her from Foal of the Foam. The smaller ship had come alongside for provisions. Boys and baskets moved on ropes between the two, and Gus climbed on to the big ship to stay with Lily for the rest of the voyage.

The captain and crew of The Good Ship Good sat eating preserved goose and drinking ale quietly with their captors. After a few mouthfuls and swallows, Anwid told Bjarwulf, in an unemotional tone, that she wouldn't rest until she'd seen him hanged, drawn, and quartered.

'Ah, yes!' Lily said.

'Say that again,' Bjarwulf asked, putting a hand behind an ear as if he wanted to be sure that he heard her quite clearly.

Anwid repeated what she'd said in the same tone, a little more slowly.

Bjarwulf heard her out attentively and when she'd finished said, 'Right y'are then. Now how about a game of Eyes and Nose?'

Anwid and Delfinola looked at each other with some surprise.

'It would help to pass the time,' Anwid said.

'And may keep us from going mad, being as we are captive in the hands of wild and terrible men,' Delfinola agreed mournfully.

'Lars!' Bjarwulf bawled. 'Set up the boards!'

Lars did not appear.

'He's having one of his headaches,' Pelf said.

'Then you set it up, Pelf,' Bjarwulf ordered, and the testy Pelf did as he was told.

The smaller of the two boards which he put down in the midst of the company was as big as a shield. It had no numbers on it but six colours instead. The arrow in its middle was not fashioned by human hands from metal but was the spine of a fish, complete with skeletal head and tail, all white and bare except for one eye still in place. On the even larger board the road had its sections painted with the same six colours repeated in order up to the big last section, a circle, on which was fixed a seal's head, its bristles intact but its eyesockets empty. Now Pelf opened a purse, and tipping it over spilled on to the deck a selection of eyes. He arranged them neatly two by two in a row: seal's eyes, bear's eyes, wolf's eyes, sheep's eyes, and a pair which Anwid saw to her moral disgust could only have belonged to a man or woman, boy or girl.

Pointing to them she said sternly, 'Whose were these?'

'A Saracen's,' Bjarwulf said. 'Beautiful, aren't they?'

'You killed a man just to get his eyes as beautiful pieces for your game?' Anwid said, frowning thunderously at him.

'I never did!' Bjarwulf protested.

'No? Then you'd killed him already and only afterwards thought of taking his eyes?'

'No! I never did!'

'It has to be one or the other,' Anwid insisted.

'No it doesn't!' Bjarwulf snapped.

'What then?'

'I didn't *kill* him,' the pirate said in a tone of hurt innocence. 'I just took his eyes.'

Anwid closed her own eyes tight. 'I shouldn't have asked,' she said. 'You are a very bad man. You have a black soul. You are a thing of the night.'

'Captain, dear, these are pirates, not noble knights,' Delfinola reminded her gently, as if it might give some comfort.

'Play!' Bjarwulf said.

'We have nothing to stake,' Anwid said.

'Play for your girls,' Bjarwulf shouted, and guffawed at the idea. 'Every time you win—you or her—I'll give back one of your girls.'

He enjoyed the game, played it with some skill, but lost more often than he won. He was not the bad loser both Anwid and Delfinola fully expected him to be, bracing themselves for bellows of rage that never came. Between them, Anwid and Delfinola won back nearly half the girls.

They'd been playing for about two hours when Bjarwulf—ignoring Pelf's objections—ordered his men to broach a barrel of the plundered green wine, and he offered some to his captives. But Anwid would have none of it. 'It isn't yours and it isn't mine,' she said. 'I'll not steal the goods I'm paid to carry.' And Delfinola felt she must do as Anwid did, so she reluctantly refused the cup held out to her.

'Do you know what you could get for that barrel at Hedeby?' Pelf squeaked at Bjarwulf, pink with annoyance.

'And what would I spend the money on if not something to get drunk on?' Bjarwulf said. But he couldn't meet the eye of his critic.

Pelf clicked his tongue.

'How you do go on,' Bjarwulf sighed. 'Tut and tut yourself. I'm not sure I'll bring you on my next raid.'

'That's for you to decide,' Pelf said snootily. 'But in this business you'll always need someone to tell you what things are worth. Know anyone else?'

'I could get a Lombard,' Bjarwulf said.

Pelf snorted. 'Hoity-toity!' he said. 'Go right ahead—but I'd like to meet the Lombard who'd put up with the song and dance you lead me!'

Bjarwulf made no answer, preferring to bury his face in his huge goblet. He and his men went on swilling the green wine until they'd drunk up the whole barrel. It made Bjarwulf ever more reckless, and he lost game after game to the women. Pelf scored a line in the deck for each girl won back, watched narrowly by Anwid in case he tried to cheat.

Bjarwulf pointed to Anwid. 'Should I hold her to ransom, eh, Pelf?' he asked.

'Who'd pay it?' Pelf challenged him to say.

'No one,' Anwid said. 'You'd get nothing for me. My father has more sense than to pay ransom for me even if he could.'

'The other one's the beauty,' Pelf said. 'But she's got no one to pay for her.'

'Who or what is this fellow?' Delfinola asked Bjarwulf, pointing to Pelf. 'He tells you what to do and some of the time you listen to him.'

'He looks after my treasure,' Bjarwulf explained, lying back on his heap of plundered rugs and cushions, all of them filthy and stained yet still magnificent, and raising his jewelled cup often to his lips. 'He knows what it's worth. Weighs it, sells it. Such a head he's got for figures! And he can write it all down too. And add up numbers. I can ask him any time and he can tell me exactly how rich I am. Just like that. That's why I call him Pelf. He likes the name.'

'Will you tell me where you come from, Pelf?' Delfinola asked, forgetting that she'd refused to talk with him until he'd learnt her name.

It was Bjarwulf who answered. 'He never says. All I can tell you is I found him in London.'

'One day when I've made enough money at sea,' Pelf said, 'I'll go and live among the Lombards. I'll set up a House of my own. I'll call it … Pelf and Pelf, Accountants.'

'Accountants?' Delfinola repeated.

'Its a new profession,' Pelf said proudly. 'It'll be big in the next millennium.'

'And who's the other Pelf?'

'My wife.'

'You're married?'

'Not yet.'

'You plan to marry?'

'Now that I've met the right woman I do.'

'You've recently met the right woman?'

'Very recently. Tonight, in fact.'

'Tonight? You've taken a fancy to one of my gels?' Anwid quizzed him sternly.

But Pelf just looked mysterious.

This dull prattle sent Gus and Lily to sleep. They lay side by side, gently rocked by the sea, the mast creaking comfortably above them. When the sun rose, its shadow glided rhythmically to and fro across their faces.

Lily stirred and flung an arm over her eyes as a long finger of light poked at them. She sat up and through half-closed eyelids regarded the sleeping figure of Gus.

'He has the build of a warrior,' she thought admiringly, and enviously. 'Women are not made to fight as men are.'

His shirt was open. His chest, heaving with each deep breath, was bared to the waist. Rising and falling on it, reflecting the light, was something made of glass and metal. 'Is it—?' Lily whispered to herself. 'Are those—? Yes, they are! Mordec's glasses. Why has Gus got them?'

She shook him awake.

'Come on, wake up!' she said urgently, but not too loudly. 'Where's Mordec?'

'What? What is it? What are you talking about?' Gus mumbled, trying to gather his thoughts as he sat up.

'Those,' Lily said, 'what are you doing with them?'

'These?' he said. 'I found them. I must remember to give them back to Mordec.'

'Why didn't you?'

'I don't know where he is. I looked for him but I couldn't find him.'

'Are you telling me he's not on the small ship?'

'He isn't. I'm sure he isn't. Are you telling me he's not here on the big ship?'

'He isn't,' Lily said, and got to her feet. 'Someone,' she went on, 'was sitting in Foal of the Foam wearing glasses when you lot scuttled The Good Ship Good. If it wasn't Mordec wearing them, who was it?'

Gus shook his head. But Lily, looming between him and the sun, was not convinced of his ignorance. She put her fists on her hips, narrowed her eyes, and said ominously, 'Was it you, Gus? Did you put on Mordec's glasses so everyone would think he was on board?'

'Why do you think I'd do that? And where are you going?'

'I'm going to Bjarwulf,' she said. 'He'll have to tell Mordec's father and mother that he's lost.'

'*Land!*' the Look-out shouted, and the cry was taken up round the ship by the pirates, and echoed by younger voices from Foal of the Foam, 'Land! Land!'

Lily looked up and saw the shore of England. She ran to help the pirates row her home.

# on felldown sands

Bjarwulf took his ships into a secluded cove, a few miles south of Loosemouth where the River Loose drools into the sea.

'My maps don't name this place,' Bjarwulf said to Anwid. 'What d'you call it?'

'Felldown Sands,' she said, 'in my father's earldom.'

'So,' Bjarwulf said, smiling and spreading his arms to show what a generous man he was, 'I've brought you safely home. You see, I believe you when you say that your father would never pay a ransom for you.' He turned to Pelf to placate him. 'I know these English, Pelf, really, they've got no heart, no human feelings. I tell you an English earl would sooner give away his daughter than his favorite hunting dog.'

'But what about her?' Pelf said, pointing to Delfinola.

'She says no one would pay for her either.'

Pelf blurted out, 'I will.'

'You?'

'I'll pay one quarter the usual.'

'Half,' Bjarwulf haggled.

Pelf considered.

'Come on, come on,' Bjarwulf said. 'Make up your mind. I haven't got all day. And it's not often

I give you the chance of keeping something for yourself.'

Delfinola's eyes were fixed on Pelf in astonishment. He met her gaze.

'If I buy you, will you marry me?' he asked.

'I would have to know you a good deal better before I could be answering that,' she replied archly. 'So be warned now—if you buy me you'll be taking a gamble.'

'Agreed,' Pelf said, and solemnly shook hands with her.

'Marry her!' Bjarwulf squeaked, and he spat. 'Marry her when you don't have to? Odds-bods, man!'

'You said you'd sell her to me, so what I do with her is my business.'

'O sure, sure. But I just want you to know that I really resent this, Pelf. I really feel let down.'

'Why? I'll still come on raids with you.'

'Will you now?' Delfinola said, eyeing him dangerously.

'You see, you see?' Bjarwulf squealed. 'I knew it!'

'Listen to me, Bjarwulf,' Pelf said, shaking a forefinger at him. 'If we don't get going we'll be spotted from the shore.'

Still looking sulky, Bjarwulf gave in. 'Well, back to work then. Ask the boys which girls they want to keep. We have to give a lot of them back but they can choose which ones to take with us.'

'Keep? Did you say *keep*?' It was Pelf's turn again to become shrill with indignation. 'Are you mad? You must sell them to Svavar the Slaver.'

'Sure. Don't get so worked up. Of course I will. Eventually. But what's the hurry?'

Lars interrupted. 'Svavar isn't keen on taking English slaves this year. Especially not girls. He told me. He's got more than he can unload.'

Pelf said, 'Now you mention it, he told me that too. Tut and tut! It's a nuisance. If we hang on to them until the spring to find another buyer, there's no way we'll get back the cost of their keep.'

'So what shall I *do*?' Bjarwulf bawled, banging the sides of his head with his fists.

'Keep calm. I'm thinking,' Pelf said. 'Don't make me deaf. Right, this is what I advise. If the boys want them as slaves or wives, fine. If not, let them go.'

'Let them go?' Bjarwulf croaked hoarsely. 'You shock me, you know that?'

'But you were the first to say it!' Pelf protested, raising both arms above his head. 'Odds-bods! You pay me for my advice, so why not take it?'

'Well, if you're sure. Are you sure? Then go and tell the boys.'

'Lars,' Pelf said, 'you heard.'

Lars waded over to Foal of the Foam, where silence fell as the students of piracy listened to the instructions from Bjarwulf. Their first reaction was to cheer, then they fell to quarrelling. Eventually they agreed on their choice and the unwanted girls were told to go.

Some of the rejected ones cried, and some of the chosen gloated a little. When Lars reported this to Bjarwulf, the pirate captain shook his head in amazement. 'There's no understanding women,' he said. 'Let's get underway.'

Anwid and her saved or rejected girls jumped overboard into the shallow water and waded ashore.

Lily appeared suddenly in front of Bjarwulf and asked, 'What do you Vikings do when one of you betrays and tries to kill another?'

Bjarwulf said, 'We put him on trial. We take him before the Thing to be judged.'

'You would do that?'

'Of course,' Bjarwulf said, 'I'm known as a man who is strict for the law.'

Anwid embraced Delfinola sadly. 'I hope you'll be happy, dear,' she said, trying not to sound too dubious.

'Time will tell, dear,' Delfinola said, eyeing Pelf again, but this time with a softer and more considering expression. 'And don't you worry now. You'll make many a voyage yet, and we shall meet again.'

Lily too embraced Delfinola and wished her happiness.

Then she went to Lars and asked him quietly, 'What happens if someone's found guilty when he's tried by the Thing?'

'Guilty of what?' Lars asked.

'Of trying to kill another Viking?'

'Who did that? What other Viking?'

'Any other. Just tell me please,' Lily said.

'Well, if he's found guilty, the one he tried to kill will choose the punishment,' Lars said.

'And if he really did kill him?'

'Then the kin of the dead man will choose the punishment.'

'Can they ask for the killer to be killed?'

'No.'

'What's the worst they can do?'

'Make him their thrall for the best years of his life.'

'Would he be allowed to go to war?'

'That's as they decide.'

Lily nodded thoughtfully. Finally, she went to Gus and spoke to him loudly, wanting others to hear.

'I know what your passions could drive you to, Gus son of Hakon. If you did what I think you did, there's nothing I can do to save you. Or defeat you. We may not meet again even on the battlefield.'

'What are you talking about?' Gus said. 'I'm coming with you. We said we would come with you. Take you home, before we start for home ourselves.'

'Mordec and you, yes. But not you without him, Gus. Stop, I said! Don't try to come with me.'

She had a Viking dagger in her hand. (Given to her by one of the pirates, he thought, or—more likely—she'd simply taken it.)

He made no move, and no one else was watching or listening.

'This isn't the time or place,' he thought, 'for us to fight each other.'

Satisfied that he wouldn't follow her, she put the dagger in her belt and left the ship. As she waded to the shore, she heard Delfinola calling after her, 'Lily—Queen Lily—where is Mordec? Will he not keep you company to your home?'

She looked back. 'No, Delfinola. Neither Mordec nor Gus will be coming home with me. But I'll not be alone. I'll start today gathering my forces.'

Captain Anwid and her girls watched the pirate ships move smoothly away with rhythmically dipping oars.

'I didn't see Mordec to wish him farewell,' she said. 'I'd have thought he'd come and look for me. And Gus—I saw him, I even waved, but he just stood there looking glum.'

The girls said nothing. They too just stood there looking glum.

'Never mind, here we are safe and sound,' the Captain went on.

Her sprightlier tone did nothing to light up the girls' faces, but she refused to notice their grumpiness.

'I promise you all will be well now. My father bathes here every morning of the year, come rain, shine, wind, hail or snow. We'll start for Cogg Hall, and likely meet him on the way.'

So they plodded over the sand, the girls having nothing to say to each other, and some of them sniffing more than usual.

Before long they saw a man approaching, on a high well-groomed horse. The Earl of Felldown. He was followed by two servants, one a long sleek fellow on a glossy ginger mare, the other, rather tousled, bouncing on a shaggy pony.

Dismounting, the Earl frowned. What were other people doing on his usually private beach? A fuss of women. And one of them was coming towards him.

'Damn,' he complained under his breath, but aloud he said, 'Good morning. I say, you bear a remarkable resemblance to my daughter!'

'I *am* your daughter, Daddy. These are my crew, or what's left of them. And over there is Queen Lily of the East Fenreach.'

'The East Fenreach? Queen? Then I know her mother, Bertha. Or her grandmother, more likely—marvelous woman. But what happened to the rest of your gels? And where's your ship, my dear?'

'It's a long story,' Anwid said. 'We were captured by Vikings. I'll tell you the rest over breakfast at the castle. Have your swim. We'll go ahead.'

'Why is the Queen standing there looking out to sea?' the Earl wondered aloud as he padded over the sand, shedding most of his garments.

Anwid supposed that Lily was thinking of her two Viking friends out on the grey-green channel.

'After all,' she said to herself, 'they've been together for months, the three of them. It's only natural for her to miss them now. But here she comes.'

'Will you go in search of your ship, Captain?' she asked.

'I will,' Anwid said. 'Why do you ask?'

'I think Mordec is still on her.'

The Captain surprised herself by exclaiming 'Oddsbods!' as she'd heard the Vikings do.

'Wasn't he on one of the pirate ships?'

Lily shook her head.

Anwid remained thoughtful for a while, then said: 'Adam the Lombard paid me to get him safely to

England. I must search for him as well as my ship. Lily, if I went in search of The Good Ship Good, would you want to come too?'

Again Lily shook her head. 'I've put off doing what I've got to do long enough.'

Anwid nodded. 'I understand.'

'Will you get together a troop of strong and fearless fighters after you find your ship and Mordec, and bring them to join my army? Not Mordec, of course.'

'I will bring myself and my gels.' Captain Anwid promised.

# castaway

Smoke was thickening in the low dark hatch when Mordec woke, coughing and gasping for breath, his whole body boiling in its own sweat. His eyes were smarting, his glasses were gone. On his head his fingers found a lump of concentrated pain where someone or something had struck him hard. Air, air—all he wanted was to get out to the air. The acrid smoke scraped his throat, almost choked him. Gasping faster, finding breath ever more difficult to draw, he crawled about feeling for the doors. Ah, here—push. Push harder. Why aren't they opening? Some rigid thing was pressing against them on the outside. He was in a trap. The ship was on fire, and he was trapped!

He banged his fists on the boards, tried to shout, but made only a thin high whimpering noise.

He banged and banged, protesting, 'No, no, no!'

Was this his fate, to die here, gasping for air, slowly burning?

'No, no, no, no, no!'

He stopped banging. For a few moments he was so gripped by terror he couldn't move. But then, forced by the very extremity of his condition, he ordered himself to 'keep calm and *think*'.

'Think what to do. Think, something is blocking the doors. Whatever it is, it can be pushed away. Push harder.'

Strengthened by terror and determination, he put his back to the doors, then his shoulder, then his back again, holding his breath in aching lungs, and—Oh! with a sense of infinite relief—he felt—yes!—whatever was blocking the doors move a little. Only a very little. But now he knew he would get out.

Again he put his shoulder to work, squeezed his stinging eyes tight shut and pressed against the doors with all his might. Again the thing shifted. He faced the doors, put his hands flat on them and pushed until his arms shook. He was using all the strength of his body, all the power of his desperation, and the thing jerked, scraped, jerked, scraped, yielding inch by inch, and one of the doors swung suddenly open all the way, letting daylight in, and him out.

Out, free, clambering to his feet, coughing as if he would bring his lungs up.

Alive. Saved.

With scalding, watering, purblind eyes he looked about him, seeing little more at first than the blur of the light itself. Slowly he made out the bare scorched deck, heaps and trails of smoking ashes, and overhead a line of busy flame where something—the remnant of a sail?—was still alight.

Hoarsely he tried again to shout, and this time a kind of shrill cry issued from his throat. He listened for an answer, for any human sound, but none came.

Infinitely glad to be alive, he stood awhile just breathing.

But all too soon distress returned as he fully grasped the peril he was in. With no crew, no sails, the ship on which he stood was adrift on the open sea.

Damaged and despoiled, it was moving, with less of a roll than usual, away from the rising sun. So surely towards England? He hoped so. But if there was land ahead, he was unlikely to see it, he supposed, until he ran into it.

The first thing he saw as clearly as the pale light and his own short-sightedness would let him, was the object which had blocked the doors: a barrel. It changed in an instant from most hated enemy to best beloved friend, for it was full almost to the brim with rainwater. He scooped a handful and drank. It was warm, tasted a little of ash and was slightly gritty, but still it was wonderfully good.

Next he explored the ship. She was hot and smoky but no longer burning.

A mast had been reduced to a charred stump, and the long handle of the rudder was charcoal, but for the most part, the tight timbers, well soaked by the storm, had resisted the fire.

He wondered why the pirates had wanted to destroy rather than take her.

The only moveable things that remained on deck, as far as he could then discover, were the water-barrel, a ladle, and some rolling tin lanterns. Everything else, every cask, box, pot, tool, garment, bundle, bag, weapon, implement, garment, was gone. His books were gone, his bundles, his cloak, his scrip. The small boats were gone, and the oars. The cargoes and stores of food were gone except for a few heads of garlic.

He wasn't hungry, but he peeled a few cloves and chewed them in the hope that they might do some medicinal good to his sore throat.

Sitting by the useless rudder, he lifted his face to the sun, and tried to think what enemy had deliberately stunned him and shut him in—had meant, in fact, to kill him—and why. Who had reason to want him dead? Olaf, because of their quarrel over Foal of the Foam? Unlikely. Olaf had seemed pleased to see him. Who then? Who hated or feared him, bore him a grudge? Someone avenging the death of Forl? There could hardly have been such a person among the women on The Good Ship Good, and certainly not among the pirates. And why hadn't Gus and Lily looked for him before sailing away? Perhaps they'd settled down in the longship and thought he was in Foal of the Foam, or the other way about.

Promising himself that he would find out the answers to all these questions, he turned his thoughts to more urgent matters.

How far away was England?

By the measure of how long it would take to drink up the water in the barrel, was landfall less or more than a barrel away?

He remembered that before the ship was blown off course, Captain Anwid had expected to be 'home by morning'. But that told him nothing useful as he had no idea how far off course, and in what direction, the storm had carried them, or how long he'd been adrift.

The sun crossed the sky and sank away, and though his head throbbed, he slept, stretched out on the cooling deck.

Next day he searched the holds again, fore and aft, feeling his way round them inch by inch. This time he found two hooded oil-soaked capes, a piece of rope, some slugs, and one of his own fishing rods which he greeted like an old friend, talking to it as he strung it with strands from the rope, calling it 'Life-saver', 'Brother', and even 'Gift of Odin'.

He fashioned a hook from a piece of a broken lantern and baited it with a slug.

And so as The Good Ship Good flew on, her lone mariner subsisted on sooty water, raw fish of several types, and garlic. One of the fish must have had poison in it. For a night and a day Mordec lay writhing and sweating, vomiting until there was nothing left in him but black bile, which came up with such a wrenching that he thought all his innards must come with it.

'Don't go and die now, when you saved yourself from something much worse!' he commanded himself in his distress: and later, feeling well enough to laugh again, 'Don't stuff your face with whatever comes along, you greedy fool!'

Now that his throat was less sore he talked aloud to himself in order to hear a human voice.

'If I don't hit England or any of the Western islands, I suppose I'll just go on, across the Blue Moor, the biggest ocean of the world they say. Sam says that India lies on the far side of it and there might be islands in the ocean.'

Rain fell. Naked and laughing, he danced in it. His clothes, spread on the deck, became so sodden that their dark blue looked black; and while they were wet he beat them with the ladle, imagining this would save them from shrinking or stiffening as they dried in the sun. And whether or not because of the ladle, they did feel softer and smell fresher than ever they had before.

The refreshed water in the barrel tasted cleaner and cooler than any he could remember.

But hope, and even his gift for laughter, weakened as the days and nights went by. He pictured the ways he might meet his end: by shipwreck, drowning, thirst, or in the jaws of a sea-monster; and while none seemed quite as terrible as the death he'd saved himself from—by suffocation, or, as he'd most feared, by burning—they were far from a joke.